He was silent for a
finger over the sca

"You said the first time you caught a bullet. How many?"

"The other night made four. I also took one in my right arm and one in my left thigh. Barely missed the femoral artery. I don't know why I keep cheating death, but there will come a day when I don't."

Efren took Selina's hand and tightened his around it. "It's my job to keep you alive, and I take that responsibility seriously. You need to get as much rest as possible. I don't know when we'll have to move next." He waited for her to get comfortable before he pulled the blanket over her. "Rest now and let your body heal."

"It may not matter," she whispered. "If they find me, all the healing in the world won't help me."

"Not if I have anything to say about it," he whispered, and her tired mind grasped onto that and vowed never to let it go.

THE
MASQUERADING

KATE WALKER

THE MASQUERADING TWIN

KATIE METTNER

Harlequin

INTRIGUE

Harlequin®
INTRIGUE™

Recycling programs
for this product may
not exist in your area.

ISBN-13: 978-1-335-45707-3

The Masquerading Twin

Copyright © 2024 by Katie Mettner

 Harlequin Enterprises ULC
22 Adelaide St. West, 41st Floor
Toronto, Ontario M5H 4E3, Canada
www.Harlequin.com

Printed in Lithuania

MIX
Paper | Supporting
responsible forestry
FSC® C021394

Katie Mettner wears the title of "the only person to lose her leg after falling down the bunny hill" and loves decorating her prosthetic leg to fit the season. She lives in Northern Wisconsin with her own happily-ever-after and wishes for a dog now that her children are grown. Katie has an addiction to coffee and Twitter and a lessening aversion to Pinterest—now that she's quit trying to make the things she pins.

Books by Katie Mettner

Harlequin Intrigue

Secure One

Going Rogue in Red Rye County
The Perfect Witness
The Red River Slayer
The Silent Setup
The Masquerading Twin

Visit the Author Profile page at Harlequin.com.

CAST OF CHARACTERS

Selina Colvert—Her past has returned from the dead to hunt her. Selina has to stay off the radar if she wants to remain alive.

Efren Brenna—He prides himself on keeping people safe. Tasked with protecting one of their own, Efren wonders if this will be the job he fails at.

Ava Shannon—Ava is proof that only the good die young. She's returned from the dead, but why is the question.

Medardo "The Snake" Vaccaro—Kingpin of the Chicago Mafia with an ax to grind with Selina and now Secure One.

Randall Loraine—He may be behind bars, but that doesn't mean he's not pulling the strings.

Kai Tanner—A man from Selina's past who may have the answer to her future.

Chapter One

"Getting shot sucks," Selina grumped, shifting to find a more comfortable position. "What's worse is this damn hospital bed. It's like a board with sheets."

Efren glanced up from his crossword puzzle and raised a brow. "Next time, don't walk in front of a bullet."

Her eye roll was epically dramatic. She noticed her reflection in the mirror across from her bed and gave herself a score of twelve out of ten. The airtime before those drugged-up eyes returned to center had earned her the two extra points.

"If I recall correctly, I didn't, but I'll keep that in mind. What were you and Eric whispering about while everyone else tried to save my life?"

His sigh was notably a six out of ten on the exasperation scale. "Has anyone ever told you that you're incredibly dramatic?"

"Not before today. It must be a new skill. You didn't answer my question."

"Nothing," he said pointedly. This time, he didn't even look up from the crossword puzzle.

"Seemed like a lot of nothing considering the time it took. I was surprised you parted ways without a hug or a secret handshake."

When he lifted his head, agitation was written all over his face. Good, she was getting to him. Maybe he'd finally leave her hospital room for more than ten seconds. "Is this contrary banter supposed to convince me to leave?" She raised a brow as an answer. "You'll have to try harder. I've protected kids with more game than you've got."

He was so irritating! Selina forced herself to take a deep breath, or at least as deep as she could without pain.

Don't let him see you sweat. It's bad enough he sees you in pain. He doesn't need to know all your weaknesses.

Efren Brenna had been a burr in her side since the day he started working for Secure One. He'd moved down a spot now that she had a bullet wound in her side, but at least that would heal and the pain would disappear. Not the case with Brenna, it appeared. His reputation was that of a hero, and his ego matched. Okay, that wasn't fair. He was a hero. He'd saved countless lives while bleeding out from a traumatic leg amputation. On the other hand, his ego was too big for her liking. It filled up the room and left no space for anyone else. At least that was her story, and she was sticking to it.

She studied the man who sat engrossed in the newspaper crossword puzzle. Selina knew he was also paying full attention to everything around him in the hospital room and the hallway. She could see his profile from her bed, and she had to admit that some might consider him handsome. His brown hair was cut short in the back with a swoop of hair over his forehead. His skin was the perfect shade of desert tan, and his brown eyes were giant with lashes that any woman would kill for. He was tall to her five and a half feet, but thin and wiry. Under his left pant leg, he wore a high-tech above-knee skin-fit prosthesis with a running blade attached. He always wore his blade when they went on missions, and since he hadn't returned to Secure One, he hadn't changed into his everyday leg. She suspected Eric would return with it soon but wouldn't ask. She didn't want him to think she cared one way or the other about his comfort when she was the one in the hospital bed.

"If you must know," he said, setting the paper aside and leaning forward in his chair, "we were talking about the case—"

Motion caught her eye and she peered through the narrow window in the door. What she saw had her heart rate climbing fast. She put her finger to her lips, her gaze glued to the nurses' station outside her door. Efren swung his head around slowly. Selina wondered if he saw her, too. If she was real. A woman with long blond hair that fell in waves against her back where it blended into her white fur coat stood tapping her bloodred nails on the counter. The door was open a crack so they could hear the discussion between the nurse and the woman.

"I'm looking for Eva Shannon. I was told she was brought to this hospital."

"I'm sorry," the nurse said. "I can only give out information to family. Are you a direct family member?"

"Yes, I'm her sister," the woman answered in a rather bored tone.

Efren raised a brow at Selina in question, and she swallowed hard. There was no way that woman was her sister. She'd put her sister in a body bag eight years ago.

"Let me check," the nurse said, typing into the computer. "I'm sorry, but I don't have an Eva Shannon on this floor. You could try two floors up. That's Med-Surg. She might be there since that's overflow when our floor gets full."

"I'll do that," the woman said.

Selina recognized the signature sass, and sweat broke out on her brow as the woman turned and sashayed toward the elevator. That woman was her sister. The one who was supposed to be dead.

Efren stood by the door until he heard the elevator's ding, then closed the door the rest of the way, jammed a chair under it and spun on her. "Get ready. I'm going to let Eric know we're moving."

"Get ready? Moving? I just had surgery to remove a bullet from my gut. I'm not going anywhere!"

Efren stalked to her bed in a way she'd never seen him move before. A lion patiently hunting prey came to mind. When he stood over her, his entire demeanor had changed. "Did you hear who that woman asked for?"

Selina swallowed before she answered, afraid nothing but a scream of terror would leave her lips if she didn't. "Eva Shannon. I don't know who that is, so I don't know what you're so worried about, Efren."

He braced his hands on the bed and leaned in until he was inches from her face. "You wanted to know what Eric and I were whispering about earlier?" He raised a brow, and she nodded. Having him this close to her was unnerving, and she blinked, afraid to breathe. "It was about the moment before you were shot. Randall Jr. said Ava Shannon right before he put a bullet in you. It was a question, not a statement. Vic also kept mumbling about you being dead, which tells me two things. That woman out there is Ava Shannon, and the woman I'm staring at is Eva Shannon. Cute play on the names. I give your mom props for that. I don't need to know the rest right now, but I need you to stop playing games. Let that fear you keep trying to swallow down motivate you to get up and get out of here before they finish the job!" The growl of exclamation was intense before he turned and picked up his bag, pulling out an encoded phone all Secure One operatives used.

With the phone to his ear, he stared her down, and she closed her eyes because if looks could kill, he'd do a better job than Randall's bullet had. The woman from a few moments ago filled her mind as terror shot through her soul. It was like looking in a mirror in a house of horrors. Ava was supposed to be dead. Selina had been the one to shoot her in the chest. The ME had assured her the bullet had done the trick and ended her reign of terror—all evidence to the contrary. Ava was alive and well, wearing her signature fur. That meant one thing. She was out for blood. Ava did not take well to being wronged, especially by her family.

Her mind warred with what she had just seen and what it already knew. How? Where had she been all these years? That night, the night they raided Randall Loraine's home, things hadn't gone as planned, but Selina wasn't sad to put her twin in a body bag at the end of the night, even if it put a target on her back.

"Listen, Eva, we have to talk about your sister," her police chief said as they strapped on their vests and readied their weapons.

"What's to talk about?" she asked, tightening the straps.

"You can't be a risk to the lives of the team. If she's going to distract you, you need to stand down."

"You should know me better than that by now," she answered, and then lined up with the rest of the team.

Eva could only hope her sister was inside those four ostentatious walls. The task force could prove she knew about the counterfeiting ring, but not that she had her hands in it. She did. They'd find that proof tonight. There was no way Ava Shannon-Loraine would let her husband run the ring alone. She was too controlling—too diabolical—to let an opportunity to manipulate and dominate Randall Sr. pass her by. They should both be behind bars, but first, they had to find the proof. Once they did, Eva had no problem being the one to put Ava in handcuffs.

The team spread out around the perimeter of the Loraine mansion. It had so many doors to cover that they'd had to pull in the SWAT teams from two separate counties. The last thing they wanted was for Randall or Ava to escape and disappear when they'd been building a case against them for over a year. If they went underground, they'd be in the wind forever.

Intel told them the couple spent their evenings in the library. Eva snickered to herself. She was the intel. She's spent enough time inside the mansion to know Ava and Randall's routine. Their sniper on the hill had confirmed they were there. That meant entering the front door, turning right down a hallway, and right into the first door. The room was small, which left them little room to hide, but Eva suspected they had a way out that even she didn't know existed.

With a nod from the chief, they rammed their way

*into the house from both ends. Eva tried to tune out the
shouting and shrill alarm as she swung into the room
where her sister and brother-in-law sat enjoying a glass
of bourbon they'd bought with blood money.*

*"Freeze! You're under arrest!" her chief yelled at
Randall as he crawled through a hatch in the floor.*

*Two SWAT guys hauled him out before he could shut
it and handcuffed him before he got a word out. Eva
swung her gun around the room. "Where is she?" It
wasn't a question as much as a rebel yell at the man
who had somehow helped her twin escape.*

*"Tag, you're it. Run, run as fast as you can, big sister,
but little sister can't be caught." Randall's words were
spat at her with so much distaste it made Eva laugh.*

*"You don't know me very well then, Randall." She
swept her gun and flashlight down the hatch, but her
twin was nowhere in sight. She didn't let that stop her.
Eva's feet barely touched the ladder's rungs before she
jumped onto the concrete floor below. The tunnel only
went one way, so on instinct, she ran, knowing it was
leading her toward the property line to the south. Ava
couldn't have that much of a jump on her. Maybe thirty
seconds. How far could she get in that time? With her
gun tight to her chest, Eva noticed movement ahead of
her. The swish of long blond hair as she climbed a ladder before popping out into the night.*

*"Ava, stop! You're surrounded!" she yelled to her
twin, but Ava didn't stop.*

*The adrenaline had Eva's legs and heart pumping as
she ran full out toward her twin, knowing that if she escaped, Eva would never be safe. She'd always have to
look over her shoulder for a bullet that one day would*

come. Ava believed in an eye for an eye, but if her family betrayed her, she would burn down the world.

Eva reached out, her fingers grasping Ava's long hair. She pulled her backward and to the ground, where she landed with an oof. "Stay down!" Eva yelled, pointing her gun at Ava's center mass.

"What are you going to do, sis? Shoot an unarmed woman?"

"If she doesn't stay down, I won't hesitate," Eva growled. Her body shook with anger, but her gun remained steady.

"What happened to you?" Ava asked, shaking her head in disdain.

"What happened to me? I'm not the one on the wrong side of the law, Ava."

"You think you're holier than thou because you're a cop. You have no idea what real life is like for me. You're about to find out."

Ava launched herself at her twin but didn't get far before Eva squeezed the trigger. The bullet knocked her back, and shock filled her eyes as she glanced down at her chest, where blood turned her white cashmere sweater bright red.

"You shot me," she hissed, that shock turning to fury. "I can't believe you shot me!"

"I warned you," Eva said, her gun still pointed at her twin. With one hand, she pushed the button on her walkie. "I need EMS on the south side of the property. I have Ava Loraine. She has a bullet wound to the chest."

"Selina!"

She started at the name, opening her eyes to stare right into Efren's brown ones.

"Sorry, what did you say?"

"I said it's time to get you up and dressed. We have to go."

There was a knock on the door, and Efren had his gun out and was next to the door before she saw him move. He opened the door a hair, but Selina couldn't see who it was.

"Quickly," he whispered, and opened the door wide enough for a nurse to slide through. He had the door shut and the chair under the handle before the nurse made it to the side of her bed.

"I have your discharge papers," she said cheerily, as though there wasn't a man with a gun in her room.

"Discharge papers?" Selina asked, her heart pounding in her chest as she pushed herself up in the bed.

The nurse shook the papers in her hand. "Everything you need to finish your recovery elsewhere. Eric told us to be alert for anyone asking about you who looked suspicious," she explained as she busied herself with the machines by Selina's bed. "When that woman looked exactly like my patient, I decided chances were good that was who he was referring to. I know you're an APP, so I'm confident you can take care of your wound, correct?"

Selina nodded, and the nurse smiled. "Good, let's get your IV out and find you something to put on that's a little less memorable." The nurse turned to Efren. "I have enough medication for the day, but she will need more than this."

Efren dug in his bag and pulled out a slip of paper. "Call it into that pharmacy, under that name. We'll pick it up."

The nurse stuck it in her pocket and set about removing Selina's IV and checking her wound. The drugs had made her head hazy, but she forced herself to concentrate. Her twin had returned from the dead, and now Selina and Efren were in her crosshairs. Her gaze drifted to Efren, his backpack on and ready to go while he glared at her in confusion and anger. She was going to have to trust him to keep her safe, but she suspected she was anything but when it came to Efren Brenna.

Chapter Two

Efren's gaze bounced between his mirrors, the road and the woman beside him. Getting her out of the hospital had been a dangerous endeavor that wasn't over yet. This old Jeep bought them time but not safety. It was registered in a way that would take someone more than a few minutes to figure out that Secure One owned it. It would get them where they needed to go, but then it would have to go.

They hit a bump, and he noticed Selina grimace. She was white as a sheet but holding on, and he couldn't ask for more than that. Efren didn't know if it was the pain or seeing her twin again that stole all color from her cheeks, but he would guess it was a little of both. She'd have to tell him exactly what they were dealing with, but it could wait until they weren't running for their lives.

"What's an APP?" he asked, hoping to distract her. She glanced at him in confusion, and he motioned behind him. "At the hospital. The nurse said you were an APP."

"Oh, I already forgot. I'm a little stressed."

"Understandable," he said with a nod.

"It means advanced practice paramedic. I can provide

extensive and advanced patient care on critical patients in the field or in an emergent disaster situation."

"I see. I guess I thought you were a nurse."

"That's what they call me at Secure One to put the guys at ease."

His laughter filled the cab of the small Jeep. "I don't think the guys need to be put at ease when it comes to you taking care of them. Not after the way you cared for Marlise, Charlotte and Bethany. It's easy to see you only want what's best for your patients."

He noticed the shrug from the corner of his eye, but she didn't say anything, so he thought it best to change the subject. "We've been on the road for ninety minutes and haven't picked up a tail, which is reassuring. We're about ten minutes from where we'll pick up your prescriptions, and then it's another thirty to the safe house."

"It's going to be tough to move," she said, her breath tight when she spoke. "Wheelchair or no wheelchair."

He nodded and squeezed her shoulder briefly before putting his hand back on the wheel. "The pharmacy has a drive-through and no monitoring cameras, which is why I picked it. Is there anything else you need? The safe house is stocked with food and supplies."

"First aid supplies?" she asked, shifting in her seat. "I'm going to need gauze and tape."

He was silent as he turned off the highway into a small town. "I'm sure there are first aid supplies, but I don't know how many. Write down what you need, and I'll have them send it out with the prescriptions." He pointed at the pad of paper in the cup holder.

It took effort, but by the time they got to the pharmacy, she had a list that he passed the pharmacist through the window. While they waited, he noticed Selina eyeing him.

"Do you always have fake IDs on you?"

"Yes," he answered, his gaze grabbing hers for a moment. "We work in the kind of business that can leave us injured and on the run. If you aren't prepared, you're dead. As soon as we get the scripts, Michael Fenstad will cease to exist, but we'll have what we need until we can get back to Secure One."

The pharmacist returned to the window and handed everything out to them. Efren gave the pain medication to Selina and money to the pharmacist. As he pulled away, he motioned at the water bottle in the cup holder.

"Take one of the pain pills."

"It's too early," she said, checking the clock.

"Listen. You'll have to walk in when we get to the safe house. The wheelchair won't go over the terrain."

"Where is this place? Canada?"

"Middle of nowhere Minnesota, so just about as bad," he answered, motioning at the water again with his chin. "Take the pill now, so it's on board by the time we get there."

She hesitated only a moment longer before she followed his order. "I'm not immobile," she said defiantly. "I'm just slow-moving."

"And when you're being hunted, slow-moving is a risk factor for death. I do not want you taking another bullet under my guard. I'll never be employed again."

"We can't have that," she muttered with an eye roll that he noticed as he checked the rearview mirror.

He'd kept an eye out since they left the town behind and noticed a pair of headlights follow them out of town.

That didn't mean it was necessarily suspicious, but he couldn't risk driving to the safe house if someone followed them.

"Tag on the rudder," she said, her gaze pinned on her side mirror. "They've been there since we left town."

"Yep, I was just thinking it was time to get rid of them." Efren slowed the Jeep and waited to see if the car went around them. It didn't.

"Next idea?" she asked, glancing at him.

"I hate to do this with you in the car, but they've left me no choice. Hang on and don't scream. It throws off my concentration."

He noted the start of her eye roll right before he yanked the wheel to the right and accelerated into the turn. He had no idea where the road went, but when the car kept going, he pressed the accelerator to the floor to put some distance between them.

"Slow down. They're not following us."

"Yet," he said, concentrating on the road ahead as he drove twice the posted speed limit. "They could be turning around as we speak."

She watched her mirror and let out a rather unladylike curse when headlights turned down the road. "We can't outrun them, and we can't bail," Selina said, her words tight.

"Well, hell, you just ruined all my plans." His words were tongue in cheek, but he heard the frustration in them, too. "Can you shoot?"

"Am I dead?"

"Not yet."

"Then I can shoot. Where's your gun?"

"Take the wheel," he ordered, waiting for her to grip

it before he reached behind him and lifted a semiautomatic from under a blanket.

Selina's whistle was long and happy. "Well, look at you! You came loaded for bear. Keep this up and I might start to like you, Brenna."

She took the gun, and he took the wheel. Rather than give orders, he decided to let her make the plan. Maybe she would start to like him a little if he didn't take all the control away from her the way everyone else at Secure One did. He had to admit that he wanted her to like him, and not because of his ego. Since he returned from the war, he vowed to himself that he'd live his life without caring whether someone liked or disliked him. He was his true self all the time, except when it came to Selina. At the very least, he didn't want her to hate him. "What's the plan, Colvert?" he asked, hoping she had one and that it would stop him from thinking about how much he wished she liked him.

"They're gaining on us fast," she observed. She carefully got herself onto the Jeep floor on her knees and aimed the gun out the window. "When I say now, stomp the brakes. When I say go, hammer it. In between those two words, duck, cover and pray."

Efren couldn't help it. He smiled. Then the first bullet smacked into the back of the Jeep.

"Guess there's no time like the present. Now!"

Efren stomped the brake as she let the first rounds go. He couldn't see if she gained any purchase while he tried to keep the Jeep from careening off the road. Another round of bullets slammed into them, taking out the back window and leaving a sucking wind on his back. The enemy was outgunned, but Selina had little time to prove it.

"Don't mind if I do," she yelled, resting the gun on the back of the seat and pulling the trigger, releasing a barrage of bullets that definitely hit home. He checked the rearview mirror again and saw the car headed for the ditch and a large tree. "Go!"

He threw his arm out to brace her as he slammed the accelerator, then held her in place until their speed evened out and she could sit up again. "Great shooting, partner," he said with a shake of his head. "Once we're off this road and at the safe house, you've got some 'splaining to do."

THE BRUSH WAS thick and wanted to pull them down with every step. Selina was tired, in pain and trying to protect a surgical wound. All of that said, she would never admit to Efren that she was glad he'd made her take that pain pill. After they found their way to the safe house using back roads, they had to bury the Jeep in a grove of trees and walk in. If the people following them had a team waiting, driving into a trap out here was certain death, even with a semiautomatic. She knew who was following them, though she wasn't quite ready to share that information with her bodyguard yet. If Ava was alive, then she had the henchmen for Chicago Mafia kingpin Medardo Vaccaro at her disposal. That meant one thing—they would never stop coming for her until she, or Ava, was dead.

Known in the crime world as the Snake, but known to her and Ava as Uncle Medardo, he was less than happy when Selina's team broke up his payday by arresting

Randall Loraine and killing Ava. Why did they call him Uncle Medardo? Her father had been part of his lower management for longer than she and Ava had been alive. When her father went into debt to Vaccaro, his boss so kindly suggested that the best way to pay off his debts was to offer one of his daughter's hands in marriage to Randall Loraine.

When her father turned up dead with a cause of death as "indeterminate," that was probably also Vaccaro getting payment for his debts. Selina had been a cop long enough to know a bribe had been accepted by the ME to make Charles Shannon's death an accident. Then again, it was equally possible Ava killed their father for marrying her off. Either way, Vaccaro was once again Selina's problem.

"Please tell me we're almost there," she whispered, trying to slide through the hole in the branches he'd made for her.

"We're here." Efren pointed ahead into the dark.

She squinted but couldn't make out a structure. "All I see is rubble."

"Exactly. That rubble is the safe house. Or rather, underneath that rubble." He flipped his night-vision goggles down and scanned the area. She leaned over, bracing her hands on her thighs to keep her side from spasming.

Getting shot in the side sucked, but Selina knew she was lucky. The bullet had missed all vital organs other than her left ovary. She already knew she couldn't have children, so this would be nothing more than a scar and a memory of another successful Secure One case in a few short weeks. It would be grand if her entire body would stop hurting, though. She'd only been out of surgery twenty-four hours when her twin showed up, and since then, she'd pushed her body to its limit. If she weren't on pain pills, she'd take a stiff drink and a bed. Right about now, she'd settle for the bed.

Efren lifted his goggles and turned to her. "I don't see anyone lying in wait. Let's get you someplace a bit more comfortable. It involves a rung ladder. I'll go down first so I can help you."

"I won't even argue." She followed him through the door of the old cabin with three walls that you could consider upright compared to the back wall, which was in shambles. The roof was gone, and the wooden floor was strewn with bricks, leaves and pine needles. Old mattresses littered the floor, along with cooking pans and metal buckets.

"There's nothing here, Efren."

"At first glance," he said. He slid one of the mattresses across the floor and revealed a hatch.

"A hidden hatch. Okay, but how do we re-cover it?"

"We don't," he answered, motioning her to follow him through the hole in the back of the cabin wall. "The ground cover will hide our footprints," he whispered, helping her around behind a row of trees. "That hatch is there to throw people off."

"What's in the hatch?"

"Pipes that look real but do nothing."

He knelt, swept his hand along the ground between two trees, and lifted a heavy metal door. "This is our hatch. I'll go down first, help you, and then come back up and close it."

Selina nodded and waited for him to climb down the rung ladder. She averted her eyes, because the memory of following Ava down a ladder just like this one eight years ago assailed her. Logically, she knew it wouldn't end the same, but the fear of Ava finding her was intense enough to wipe logic off the table.

An emergency light lit the ladder, and she saw Efren setting the bags on the bunker's floor. Selina prayed she'd make it down without needing his assistance. It would be a mistake to have his hands wrapped around any part of her, and keeping her distance would be the only way to survive any type of forced proximity. She chuckled to herself. Talk about an oxymoron.

"Selina!" he hissed, and she started, forgetting where she was and what she was supposed to be doing. It must be the pain pills. It couldn't be the man waiting for her below.

"Sorry," she whispered. "I was planning out my descent."

Her eyes rolled at herself that time, but she managed to make it down the rung with minimal pain and without falling into his arms. He climbed the ladder again to shut the hatch, and she walked to a bunk bed in the room, sat down and promptly passed out.

Chapter Three

"I need your help, Kai."

Eva could see that the man in front of her was terrified, but he finally nodded. "And you're sure I won't get in trouble for this?"

"Positive," Eva promised. "You have to know I don't have any other options. I wouldn't do this if I did."

"I know, but Eva, he's going to be heartbroken. I don't know if he'll ever recover."

"Selina?" a voice asked. "Selina, wake up. You're moaning. It's time for medication."

She blinked several times as the man beside her morphed from Kai into someone else. Someone she didn't know. Had they found her that quickly? "Kai! Kai! Help!"

"Selina, relax!" the man said, his voice frantic. "I'm Efren. You work for Cal Newfellow at Secure One. Your friends are Mina, Marlise and Charlotte."

Efren. Secure One. She blinked again and swallowed down the fear before she sat up gingerly. "Sorry. I got confused."

"I understand," he said, handing her a water bottle. "I remember what that's like when you're tired, sore, taking medication and dredging up the past."

"What time is it?" she asked to change the subject. The last thing she wanted to talk about with Efren Brenna was the past, though she knew it was inevitable.

"It's two a.m. I've been in touch with Cal and taken a nap. I didn't want to wake you until you had a chance to sleep off the pain from walking in. You must be hurting."

"I've felt better, but I'm alive. I can thank you for that both times."

"We're a team, which means no thanks is needed. I wish I could have spared you the pain of getting here, though."

"We're a team, so no apology is needed," she said with a wink. "Besides, you managed to get me the medication I needed and to a safe place before daylight."

"Only because of your scary accurate marksman skills. Does Cal know you're a crack shot?"

"Yep," she answered, taking the pills he held out. After she tossed them back with a swig of water, she took a moment to take in the room. "Where are we?"

"Nice pivot, Colvert," he said with a shake of his head. She smirked and accepted the hand he held out to help her up. "This is the safe house Cal built when he realized if we continued with these kinds of cases, one day we would need it."

"I can't believe he built a replica of the bunker at Secure One."

"If it ain't broke, don't fix it," Efren said with a chuckle. "But you're correct other than the kitchen, compostable toilet and small wash basin. Everything runs on battery power, so you could stay here for a few weeks if you conserve water and power. At least we have the communication equipment available."

"With the amount of equipment here, you could run a small country," she said jokingly. "I need to use that compostable toilet, and then I suppose I need to touch base with my boss."

"Probably would be a good idea," Efren agreed with a wink. He opened the bathroom door for her. "Water, soap, towels and clean clothes are in the cabinet," he said, pointing at the metal locker next to the toilet. "When you're done, you'll tell me everything from start to finish. If I'm going to keep you safe, I have to know what's coming at us."

Fear shot through her at the idea of breaking her silence after all these years. Rather than speak, all she did was close the bathroom door.

WHO'S KAI? That was the only question running through Efren's head. He was obviously someone from Selina's past and someone she relied on when she was in trouble. Was he an ex-boyfriend or an ex-partner? It wasn't a giant leap to assume that Selina, aka Eva, was a cop in her past life. She knew too much to be anything but a cop or a criminal, and he knew Cal didn't hire criminals. He would still make her spell everything out, from her prior career choices to what happened with her sister. Until he understood what they were dealing with, there was no way for him to make a plan to keep her safe. After they talked, they'd contact Secure One as a united front.

The bathroom door cracked open, and Selina walked out. Her steps were ginger, but she'd washed up and found clean joggers in the cabinet. "I have to say, a sponge bath and clean clothes do make me feel like a new woman."

"Maybe some food would, too?" Efren turned from the small camp stove with a pan of hot soup he set at the little two-person table, along with a bag of crackers and her water.

"I hate to admit that you're right, but you're right. Thanks for fixing it for me."

"Remember what I said about thank you?" Efren asked. "Chances are there will come a time when you'll do the same for me. In the meantime, why don't you tell me what we're dealing with here?"

Rather than speak, she focused on the soup and crackers, so he patiently waited for her to finish. Finally, she lowered the spoon and motioned toward the two accent chairs in the corner by the beds.

"If I'm going to give you my life story, we may as well be comfortable. It would be smart to call Cal so I only have to do this once. He knows some, but not all, of my past."

He helped her stand and walked with her to the two chairs in the corner. Once they were comfortable, he addressed her prior statement.

"I have it on good authority that they're sleeping right now, so they can be prepared to help us come daylight. Before sunup, I need a timeline of what happened since the night your sister 'died.'" He put air quotes around that word since they both knew she was alive and well. "Give it to me as you would if you were a witness giving a statement at the station. I'll write it down so we can pull out the pertinent and important information to give the team when we talk to them in the morning."

"You're assuming I was a cop?" she asked with a brow raised.

"Am I wrong?" he asked, raising the opposite brow.

"Unfortunately, no. That said, it's been eight years since I took any witness statements, so you'll have to forgive me if I'm a little rusty." She was going for levity, so he chuckled softly.

"I've got the pad and the time," he said with a wink, motioning at the paper on his lap. "I should ask if we're breaking any contracts with the United States Marshals Service by talking about this?"

"WITSEC?" she asked, and he nodded once. "No. I'm not part of WITSEC."

"Okay, then start whenever you're ready." Efren respected that it would be hard for her to trust him with the truth when she'd kept it a closely guarded secret for so long.

She shifted in the seat, and he got up, grabbed a pillow from the bed and handed it to her. After she slid it along her side, she cleared her throat. "I'd been a Chicago cop for four years when I joined a task force tracking a counterfeiting operation. I was aiming to make detective and knew shutting down the operation would be the feather in my cap to get the promotion."

"How long ago did you join the task force?" he asked, writing on the pad rather than making eye contact. He hoped that would make it easier for her to focus.

"That would be ten years ago now," she answered. "The task force suspected that the counterfeiting originated with Chicago Mafia kingpin Medardo the Snake Vaccaro. I was already intimate with him and his business, so when they asked me to join the task force, I readily agreed."

"Had you worked a case where Vaccaro was involved before the counterfeiting?"

"Nope," she said, popping the *P* harder than necessary. "My father worked for him my entire life. Lower management, if you catch my drift."

His brows went up. "That's wild. A cop's father was a Mafia henchman."

"It wasn't easy being that cop in the beginning. When they found out about my father, my superiors tried to fire me for being a Vaccaro plant. I fought back with the union and won since there was no evidence that I was tied to Vaccaro. I had worked hard to keep myself separated from anything my father did since I was in high school. Then my father got behind on some debts to his boss. The Snake offered him an opportunity to pay them off by giving the hand of one of his daughters to be married to a man within his organization."

"And that daughter sure as hell wasn't you?"

"Nope," she said again, staring at her lap. "My father knew I was working my way to detective, and I wouldn't hesitate to arrest anyone who got in my way of accomplishing that goal, including him."

"Did your sister have her own life by then as well?"

"Nope," she said a third time, much to his amusement.

"I'm sorry for laughing, but I can't help but wonder if this entire conversation will be punctuated with the word nope."

"Nope." This time she gave him a quirky smile. "To answer your other question, Ava did not have her own life. She was a spoiled, entitled debutante wannabe who thought Daddy would bankroll her for life. She never wanted to lift a finger or work for anything. She was fifteen minutes younger than me, and we were identical twins in everything but our work ethic and morals."

"Neither of which is genetically embedded in us," Efren said, and she pointed at him.

"Well said. As a result, my father racked up debts and favors while trying to pay for Ava's every whim. Things like her multiple college degrees that she started and stopped, her spa business that never took off because she was never there, and other random nonsense that my father bankrolled. When the Snake asked for a daughter's hand, it was a no-brainer. If my father could unload Ava, he'd stay out of debt and on the right side of favor with his boss."

"I'm going to go out on a limb and guess that her betrothed was Randall Loraine Sr."

"That's him," Selina answered, practically spitting the words from her lips. "He was twenty-three years older, had three sons and was already a widower. That didn't stop her. As soon as she realized he had money, she readily agreed to warm his bed."

"So, your sister marries Loraine and ends up helping him run a counterfeiting racket?"

"That's a short jump of a long story, but it's the nuts and bolts. Ava married him twelve years ago, and I suspect, though I can't prove it, he was already running the counterfeit operation out of his mansion in Bemidji. The Snake wanted Ava there to paint Randall as the consummate family man who found love again as well as a mother for his boys. Hilarious, since those boys were already teenagers or young adults."

"What happened to your father?"

"He was found floating facedown in the Chicago

River. His death was ruled indeterminate, so I know money changed hands with that death certificate. They also didn't find any water in his lungs, which means he was dead when he landed in the river."

"Nothing fishy about that," Efren muttered, and Selina laughed.

"I can't say for certain that Ava didn't kill him and convince Randall to help her cover it up. She believes in an eye for an eye, and if family wrongs her, she will burn down the world."

"Why would she kill your father? Did he wrong her somehow?"

"I would have no way of knowing that for certain, but if Randall told her Daddy had to die, then she wouldn't hesitate to do it."

"Which explains why she came looking for you as soon as she knew where you were."

"Likely," she agreed, shifting again. She was getting tired, and he had to wrap this up before she was in too much pain to talk. "That or she always knew where I was and was biding her time. If that's the case, then she's smarter than I gave her credit for all these years."

"I doubt she was the brains behind any fake death operation." Efren felt terrible that Selina saw herself as less than her sister when she was the one standing on the right side of the law. "She would have needed help and that help had to come from somewhere."

"More like someone," Selina agreed with a nod. "Vaccaro. I was told that my twin went straight to hell. Obviously, someone got the message wrong."

"Or someone wanted you to think she went straight to hell," Efren pointed out.

"That could be if the EMTs were bought in that town. No way to know now, but I wouldn't put it past Vaccaro to reel Ava back in if Randall had been snagged. The fact that she showed her face now terrifies me."

"Tell me why," he encouraged, leaning forward to show her he was listening and interested in what she had to say. He'd been listening and interested in what Selina Colvert had to say since the day he met her. While she treated him like a second-class citizen and with as much malice as is tolerable in the workplace, he'd always known it was an act. She was scared and hurting, but kept a tight lid on her emotions so as not to rock the boat. Now he understood why. She couldn't rock the boat. If she left Secure One, her life would be in jeopardy again.

"Well, her husband is still in prison, one of her stepsons is dead, another is going to prison, and she could still face charges for the counterfeiting operation. Showing her face again puts her at risk for arrest, if they found evidence she was involved, which I have no way of knowing. My main worry is that she started warming Vaccaro's bed after her 'death' and has become another head of the snake."

"Was there evidence that she was involved in the counterfeiting operation?"

"Before we raided the mansion, we only had circumstantial evidence. You and I both know she was involved, though. She was Randall's wife and secretary. Here's the thing, Ava is lazy, but she's incredibly smart and quick on the draw."

"Just like you are."

"I suppose genetics come into play there."

"You think she knew more than she let on."

"I think she was the brains behind the operation. Randall Sr. is polished, but he isn't smart or talented when it comes to the art of manipulation, if that makes sense."

"Of course it does. He was a puppet of the Snake. A smart man wouldn't allow himself to be controlled that way."

"That sums it up. I spent a lot of time with them as a couple, and Ava ruled the roost. Not just in a spoiled wife kind of way, either. She ruled that house with an iron fist, both with Randall and the two boys still at home. All of that said, we knew the information inside the house held the answers the task force needed to put together a case against them both. I don't know if evidence was ever found to prove she was involved," Selina said with a shake of her head.

"You were on the task force, so wouldn't you know that information?"

"If I had been part of the task force after that night, yes."

"Let me guess. You were put on administrative leave for shooting your sister?"

"Bingo. I was on mandatory administrative leave until the shooting was investigated. I never heard if they found evidence of her involvement, but I know Ava, so I suspect they didn't. If she was the one running the operation, she'd make sure her hands stayed squeaky clean while Randall's were all red."

"Do you think they pulled you because they thought you were a Vaccaro plant?"

"No." Her gaze dropped to her lap before she finished. "I knew being part of that task force would put me in grave danger. I'd be lucky to survive a few days outside of police protection before they'd find me floating face-down just like my father. So I turned in my badge and gun, drove to Wisconsin, and fell off a bluff with the raging Wisconsin River below. That was the last time anyone saw Eva Shannon."

Chapter Four

Selina noted the surprise on Efren's face, but to his credit, he simply glanced up and waited to see if she would continue. When she didn't, he set the pen down on his paper.

"How about we take a break? You can hardly keep your eyes open."

She shook her head. "No. I'm fine. If we're going to call Secure One in the morning, we have to work this out. Then I can sleep."

He picked up his pen again. "You decided falling off a cliff was easier than going into WITSEC?"

"Easier? Not in the beginning. Faster? Yes, and at the time, I needed to disappear quickly. Since I didn't have any family left, it didn't matter if I was in WIT-SEC or on my own. Besides, I couldn't be sure that the Snake didn't have a plant somewhere in the marshals' office. If I took protection, then I had to trust them and probably would end up with a bullet between my eyes sooner rather than later. I trusted myself and knew I wasn't going to double-cross me."

"Valid. Still had to have been hard."

"It was. I had my search-and-rescue dog to think about. I convinced my friend Kai Tanner to take him for me and to tell the authorities I fell. Since the Wisconsin River opens up into the Mississippi, if they didn't find a body, they wouldn't be surprised."

"He was willing to lie to authorities for you?"

"He may have had a bit of a crush on me," she said. "Maybe if our lives had been different, I could have seen us together, but there was no way I was dragging someone as honest and kind as Kai into something that could get him killed."

"You could have taken the dog and run."

"I could have," she agreed with a head nod, "but then the Snake would know I'd run. Taking Zeus would have been a dead giveaway, no pun intended. It was the hardest thing I've ever had to do to hand his leash over to Kai, but Zeus deserved better than what I could give him."

"Then what happened?"

"I don't know," she answered with a shrug. "I checked the *Tribune* but since I went missing in Wisconsin, it didn't even make the papers. At least not that I could find. The Wisconsin papers reported it as the death of a search-and-rescue agent that was a tragic accident. That told me Kai didn't get in trouble for falsely reporting my death."

"Man, sucked to be him," Efren muttered, making notes.

"Why do you say that?" She snapped her head up, immediately on the defense. "You don't think it sucked to be me?"

"I know it did. It had to be a difficult decision to know your choice was to trust the institution you worked for or go it on your own. It had to be a brutal decision to hand over your dog and walk away. I was simply saying from a guy's perspective, that it sucked for Kai, too. Not only did he have to give up the woman he cared about, but he had to pretend that she was dead for the rest of his life, when he knew you were still out there. It's hard to move on with life when your heart and mind are in a different place."

"Thanks for doing a better job of gutting me than the bullet did." She wrapped her arm around her belly. "I felt like hell asking him, but I had no one, and he knew that. He wanted to be my someone any way he could, and this was the only way he could, so he stepped up."

"What happened after you 'fell off the cliff'?" He put that whole phrase in air quotes, too.

Her sigh was loaded. What followed that day was hard. Harder than anything she'd ever done, and that said a lot when she grew up with a father who worked for the Mafia.

"I was lucky to have money, several new identities and the ability to change my appearance rather easily, but it was still hard to navigate a world where you couldn't trust a soul. You couldn't stay in one place more than a day, visit the same store or restaurant more than once, or even use public transportation. I was lucky the raid happened during the summer or I would have been in much deeper trouble."

"How did you move around?"

"I stole old cars from people's yards, rode ATVs or walked."

Selina stood and paced to her left, stretching her side out carefully. She was relieved it was feeling better after the food and medication. The longer she was down and weak, the easier it was for the Snake to find a way in.

"She was dead, Efren. By the time EMS got to her, she had practically bled out."

"Did you see her code and them call her time of death?"

Selina turned back to him. "No. They ran with her to the ambulance, worked on her, and then I watched them go hands-off," she explained, holding her hands in the air near her chest. "The EMS guys waited a few moments and then one shook his head. They covered her with a sheet and told me she was gone, so they'd take her to the ME. When they pulled away, it was without lights and sirens."

Efren tapped his pen on the pad. "You didn't go to the morgue?"

"No. There was no reason to. I didn't need to identify the body since everyone knew who she was. I was busy dealing with the fallout of shooting her."

"Did they hold a service for her?"

Selina gave him the palms-out. "No way for me to know since I was gone less than twenty-four hours after it happened. I resisted the urge to google anything to do with her."

"Not even from the secure servers at Secure One?"

"Not even then." She shook her head. "You don't understand the ruthlessness that is Vaccaro, Efren. People romanticize the Mafia like they're some kind of antihero who can be redeemed with good morals and making the right choices. If only they knew these guys." She shook her head again in frustration. "They're more likely to be old fleshy men than young, sexy tatted guys in suits. They wouldn't think twice about putting a bullet in you because you're between them and their whiskey bottle. There is nothing romantic about the Mafia, and it's a dangerous ideation to lead women to believe they'd be loved or respected by one. Women are a pawn to these men, and that's why I know Vaccaro had to be involved in Ava's death and rebirth."

"I have to heed to your knowledge on the Mafia as mine is limited to movies and books, but I still agree that a kingpin only does what's best for him, regardless of who is in his way." She lowered herself to the chair and nodded. "I'll have Mina search and see what she can find in the archives."

"You're asking the wrong questions." She sat and leaned over her knees to rub her forehead.

There was no question that the surgery and medication were the reason she couldn't pull all of this information together logically as she usually would. It was frustrating. They were on a timeline that was a matter of life or death. She needed to get it together.

"I wish I knew the right questions, Selina. I'm afraid I'm a bit out of my depth here. I'm a bodyguard, not a cop," he reminded her. "You're telling the story."

Selina slumped over in the chair. "I shot her, Efren. She was dead."

"They wanted you to think she was dead. That doesn't mean she was. If you could have, I know you would have gone to the morgue and checked her cold dead body yourself, right?"

"I would have watched the autopsy." Her words held a bit more fire again, and he smiled.

"Money had to have changed hands."

"If Vaccaro was involved, then there's no question," she agreed. "What I want to know is, was there an autopsy report?"

Efren scribbled it down on his pad. "Because if there was, he paid off more than an EMT?"

"Bingo. Then it becomes a plan rather than a reaction."

"A plan instead of a reaction?"

"Think about it." She grimaced, but it wasn't physical pain. It was the kind of pain a person was in when their world was crumbling around them and they didn't know what to do. The terror inside her had filled her head to toe. There was no room left, but the terror kept coming in waves. As much as she trusted Secure One, her experience with Vaccaro told her she was a dead woman walking. "They knew the task force was closing in, or at the very least, they knew we were looking for that final connection so we could arrest them. Randall and Ava had a plan in case they were arrested or killed."

"Or gravely wounded." Selina tipped her head in agreement to his statement. "Did you keep the task force a secret?"

"From the Snake?" Efren nodded. "We didn't broadcast it, but he was used to being under investigation. It wasn't a stretch for him to know we were looking for the head of the counterfeiting ring. Are you implying there was a mole somewhere? It wasn't me."

"It never crossed my mind that you were," he assured her. "That said, I'm not implying it. I'm assuming it. The Chicago PD is vast in its size and scope. It could have been a beat cop, lieutenant, detective, secretary or janitor. Whomever it was, they were reporting your progress to Vaccaro."

"Could be. It also could be they had a plan in place for every operation he had going on, which was also vast in its size and scope. That's less important now eight years later. What is important is why did she appear now, and how did they know I was working at Secure One?"

"The timing is suspicious. I'll give you that. We already know the Winged Templar killed Howie Loraine, but he had to have Vaccaro's approval to put out the hit. Then, unbeknownst to them, Secure One got involved. Suddenly, there you were, served up on a silver platter."

"I was never visible until the night we tried to rescue Kadie and Vic at the Loraine mansion," Selina reminded him. She hung her head and sat quietly, letting the information roll through her tired, drugged mind. When Victor Loraine's girlfriend Kadie had been kidnapped by his older brother in hopes of getting his hands on Vic's infant son, Secure One had sent Vic in to talk to his brother in hopes of finding Kadie. Instead, Randall Jr. kidnapped Vic too and it was up to Secure One to rescue them. She snapped her head up with her lips in a thin line. "Randall Jr. knew Ava was alive."

"Did he look like he knew she was alive right before he shot you?"

Selina chewed on her lip for a few seconds while she ran the interaction through her mind, forcing herself not to focus on the gunshot, but the seconds before. "No, but all he said was 'you're dead.' He didn't call me Ava Shannon."

"Vic did. Vic specifically said Ava Shannon and that he saw her die."

"Think about it, Brenna." She heard the frustration in her voice, but it wasn't with him. It was with this situation that she couldn't control. "We're twins and I 'died,'" she said, using air quotes, "the day after Ava. Randall said you're dead because he knew I was supposed to be dead, too. Wait." She held up a finger as though she was replaying something in her mind. "Vic said he saw Ava dead?" Efren nodded. "Then he really was knocked silly. He hadn't been to the mansion since he left for college until the day he went there looking for Kadie. I know for a fact he wasn't there the night of the raid."

Efren immediately scratched a sentence on the page and underlined it. "That's a breakthrough."

"That Vic was knocked silly?"

"No. He may have seen her dead. There could have been a service. I'll have Mina contact him and ask about it. It would answer the question of how hard they worked to prove she was dead. Mina is great at digging until she finds those answers, so let's leave it to her. No sense in beating our heads against the wall when we have no way to find out."

Selina pointed at the computers off to her side. "But we do. A little search would give us a lot of these answers."

"It could also open us up for an attack that I can't predict. Until I know how far we can go with those machines, I can't risk it." He set his pad aside and stood, holding out his hand to her. "You've been up long enough. You need to rest. You had a hysterectomy less than twenty-four hours ago."

Selina slipped her hand in his, and the sensation was like silk. He'd touched her before, but this time was different. There was trust there that he was going to help her, even if it were as simple as getting her out of the chair without pain. He ran his thumb over the back of her hand, and the simple motion gave her silent comfort and security that just a few seconds ago she didn't feel. She would never admit it, but whenever she spoke of Vaccaro, the terror was overpowering. Efren was the only reason she wasn't rocking in a ball in the corner. She was a cop, but when you have intimate knowledge about someone as dangerous as the Snake, it was hard not to be terrified.

"Wait," she said, freezing with her hand still in his. "A hysterectomy?"

"The doctor told us he had to take an ovary and without your uterus, you can't have children. I assumed that meant they did a hysterectomy. I'm sorry, Selina. I wish you'd had more time to deal with that before we had to run."

"Time to deal with it?" She pulled her hand from his and lifted her shirt, showing him a healed starburst wound on her abdomen just outside of the bandage from her latest incision. "I'd been a cop about three weeks when I caught a bullet the first time," she explained. "That one ripped through my uterus and tore it to shreds. I was twenty-two. You don't have to worry about me coming to terms with anything. The kid card sailed for me thirteen years ago."

He was silent for a moment as he took in the scars across her belly. "The first time?" She tipped her head in confusion and he traced his finger over the scar. "You said the first time you caught a bullet. How many?"

"The other night made four and the second gut shot. I also took one in my right arm that still has shrapnel left and one in my left thigh. Barely missed the femoral artery. I don't know why I keep cheating death, but there will come a day when I don't."

He took her hand again and tightened his around it. "Not if I have anything to say about it. It's my job to keep you alive, and I take that responsibility seriously. With that responsibility comes the right to order you to bed, and that's what I'm doing. You need more sleep."

When he turned to the bunk, her hand still in his, her eyes were barely open. "I'm relieved to know they didn't remove major organs yesterday. That means you're at less risk of massive bleeding if we have to run again. You need to get as much rest as possible over the next couple of days. I don't know when we'll have to move next."

After straightening the blankets, he helped her down and waited for her to get comfortable before he pulled the blanket over her. "You'll wake me as soon as the team is ready to talk?"

"You know I will," he promised, resting his hand on her shoulder for comfort. "I'm going to doze a bit while keeping an eye on the cameras."

"That's kind of an oxymoron, Brenna," she said, her eyes almost closed and her tongue thick when she spoke. "You need to sleep, too."

"Shh," he whispered, powering down the lantern over the bed area. "Rest now and let your body heal."

"It may not matter," she murmured, and she heard the terror again. "If they find me, all the healing in the world won't help me."

"Not if I have anything to say about it," he whispered, and her tired mind grasped on to that and vowed never to let it go.

Chapter Five

As soon as Selina dropped off to sleep, Efren lowered himself to the chair next to the bunks and leaned over on his elbows to gaze at her. Since the day he'd met her, Selina had intrigued him. The push and pull between them was both frustrating and something to look forward to in his workday. What bothered him the most, though, was knowing she didn't like him. It wasn't his ego that was bothered, either. It was knowing that he *cared* that she didn't like him. A long time ago he'd promised himself he'd never care about anyone enough for their opinion of him to matter. The war taught him that caring about people ends in heartache and pain when they're taken from you in the blink of an eye. The Snake could certainly take Selina in the blink of an eye; he didn't even question that. He was an excellent bodyguard with a stellar record, but he could only do so much as one man.

Still, he had to admit he cared. He wanted to know why she hated him, and wondered if he'd done something to make her so standoffish from the get-go. Everyone at Secure One assured him that it had nothing to do with him, but he wasn't so sure about that. If nothing else, their forced togetherness might afford him the opportunity to discover why she hated him so he could set her straight and put them back on even ground. Whether it was something he could fix or not was another issue. For now, though, Selina needed sleep above all else.

His gut twisted as he stared at her gorgeous face finally relaxed in sleep. She had stolen his breath from their first meeting. Her long blond hair had been pulled back in a no-nonsense ponytail, but the waves still flowed down her back. Her blue eyes were sharp and assessing, but he could easily picture what those eyes would look like when the lights were low and she was relaxed. He wondered if she knew how much terror reflected back at him from those eyes when she spoke of Vaccaro. The answer was no because if she did, she'd use her iron will to shut that down, too. To say Selina Colvert intrigued him was an understatement.

He stood and walked to the computer screen that served as his eyes outside the bunker. The screen had four quadrants, each showing a camera view angled around the old cabin structure. All was quiet, so he clicked the mouse to check the four cameras that blanketed the woods in every direction. Those were quiet, too, other than a family of deer foraging through the underbrush.

Returning to the real reason he was here, he pondered their next move. The Snake had wrapped himself around Selina a long time ago. His goal was to snuff the life out of her to keep his secrets hidden. Efren had every intention of cutting off the head of the snake before he had the chance to do that, though. This was a case of hunting the hunter, but he was prepared to do anything to keep his body count at zero. There wasn't a chance in hell the body to break his winning streak would be hers. He'd make sure it was his body before hers. The idea of losing Selina ran a shiver of fear down his spine as a huff left his lips.

Sure, you want to protect Selina because it's your job, he told himself. *No, you want to protect her because she represents everything you'll never have. As long as she's alive, you can focus on the reasons why she doesn't like you rather than on the reasons why you like her.* Above all, he knew the main reason he wanted to focus on protecting her was to avoid thinking about why the idea of losing her made him instantly lonely. That, above all else, was an emotion he could not afford to entertain.

SELINA STAYED IN bed and watched the man across the room. He had pulled his socket off and was massaging his limb. If she knew one thing about Efren Brenna, it was that he'd never show weakness, and that meant never taking his prosthesis off. In fact, this was the first time she'd seen him take it off longer than to shower or sleep since she met him. The paramedic in her wished he was closer so she could check the skin, but since he wasn't, she'd have to trust that he'd tell her if there was a problem.

She laughed internally. As if he'd tell her anything about himself. Hard-core aloofness was a requirement to be in the boys' club at Secure One. Selina understood it, though. Everyone at Secure One, including herself, dealt with one type of PTSD or the other. You didn't go to war or work in law enforcement and not see things that changed you and stayed with you forever. You learned to compartmentalize it; once you did, you never spoke of it again. It had been heavily debated whether that was a smart way to approach it, but in the end, it didn't matter what anyone else thought was the correct answer. What mattered was getting through every single day trying to live in a society you no longer trusted.

Efren finished his towel massage and then used his pull sock to seat his limb back into the prosthesis. Her practiced eye watched and waited for his facial expression to change when he added the valve to the socket, but he appeared comfortable through the entire process. Since he wore a skin-fit prosthesis, meaning there was nothing between his limb and the socket, she made a mental note to keep an eye on his gait over the next few days. The running blade made him fast when in the field, but walking on it all day was going to be more difficult than on his leg with a computerized knee. Wearing the blade required him to use his limb differently to make the "knee" bend, and that would wear the skin in different places. She hated to admit that there was a weak link in their chain, but there was, and his leg was it. Not because he wasn't competent in his job, but because the situation they were in called for rough terrain that could damage his limb or his blade at any point and leave them vulnerable to Vaccaro.

The name bounced around her brain like a bullet, and she closed her eyes again. Vaccaro had done enough damage to her family and her friends at Secure One. She was happy that the person to take a bullet the other night was her. No one else deserved what Vaccaro doled out to get to her family. Well, namely her, since it appeared her twin was still in good favor with that monster. She and Ava were the last of the Shannon family tree, and she was never more grateful for that.

Selina didn't care what Uncle Medardo had planned for her. She'd beat him at every turn her entire life, and she had no intention of breaking that streak now. Besides, she had all of Secure One behind her, fighting for the answers she'd need before she faced him again. She hoped, anyway. Part of her knew that Secure One would have her back, but the other part worried that her fear the last few months had spread like a virus through the team. If Vaccaro sensed dissension among the ranks, he might be tempted to break them and force people to pick sides.

Since the Red River Slayer had been captured, Selina had been struggling to keep her demons hidden from everyone all the time. Caring for Marlise and Charlotte had been difficult when they first came to Secure One. They were abused and broken, and trusted no one but her. The things they told her and the scars they showed her would never leave her mind or her heart. Then Bethany arrived as they chased the Red River Slayer, and she nearly broke Selina. How did you care for someone who had been held hostage, assaulted repeatedly and groomed to be the sex slave of a madman? Cal and the team knew Bethany needed more help than Selina could give her, but they insisted she try. If only they had spent a few hours in her shoes. She might be an APP, and once a cop, but she was also a woman. She had spent the last three years caring for these women who needed her in the moment, but no one was there for her when she needed someone. That, above all else, was what hurt her the most.

When the Loraines popped back up in her life in a

way that she couldn't escape, her illusions of safety shattered. All bets were off. Her demons came out to play all day, every day, and fighting them back had become a losing battle. She should have run the moment someone said the name Randall Loraine, but she had nowhere to go. Running meant certain death. Sticking with Secure One gave her a fighting chance.

"I'm not going to let him get to you," Efren said once he stood in his socket again.

His voice startled her, and she jumped. "I never thought you would."

As he walked toward her in the bed, she'd never felt more vulnerable, so she sat up and swung her feet to the floor. "Nice try, Colvert, but your fear filled the room and stole all the oxygen. How do you think I knew you were awake?"

"Eyes in the back of your head?" The question was sarcastic, just the way she wanted it. She had to keep Efren at arm's length if she was going to get through this with any kind of dignity.

"You don't know how often I wish that were the case. How are you feeling?"

After stretching side to side and gingerly probing her abdomen, she looked up at him. "It's better this morning. It still feels bruised, but the burning pain in my gut from the incision is mostly gone."

"Good, I'm happy to hear that. It won't stay that way if you overdo it, though. While in this bunker, I need you to be down more than you're up. If we have to move quickly, you'll need your reserves to get through it. The terrain out there is tough to traverse when you're in top form, much less recovering from surgery."

"Speaking of terrain. How's the leg?" she asked, nicer this time, as she rubbed her eyes. "I noticed you had your socket off."

If he thought she didn't notice the way his eyes widened when she said that, he didn't know her very well. His "it's fine" was also not an acceptable answer.

"Run it down," she ordered. "Skin, pinch points, pain, function."

Efren threw his hand onto his hip with a huff. "I've been an amputee a long time. I don't need help with managing my situation. My leg, or lack thereof, will not be a factor in keeping you safe."

"That might be true, but I need help managing my situation, and the only help I have is standing in front of me," she said, her voice full of fire. "So run it down and be honest. I have the skills to keep small problems from becoming big problems."

"The skin is fine, there are no pinch points, I'm managing my phantom pain by keeping the limb compressed and with towel massage, and the function is superb. I could run this leg at half function and it would still be more than we'd need to get your surly backside out of trouble."

"Ego much?" She stood and straightened completely, finally able to take a deep breath.

"Honesty isn't ego."

She lifted a brow and pinned him with an assessing gaze. "I'm surprised they didn't bring your other leg to you at the hospital before they left town."

He shook his head as though he was thoroughly fed up with her questions. "Eric intended to, but Mack took mobile command back to Secure One before he got there to get it. They were headed back with it when we had to bail. It's not a problem, Selina. Walking through that terrain last night on the computerized knee would have been much more difficult. The blade is thinner and easier to maneuver in those situations. They both have their pros and cons. Well, look at you. Standing up straight is an improvement."

Selina accepted that he wanted to change the subject, so she didn't push. "The faster, the better, if you ask me."

"In this situation, yes, but don't overdo it. This is a marathon, not a sprint."

"Speaking of, have you heard from anyone?"

"Cal contacted me. They're ready to meet when we are. Mina has been working for a few hours already."

"Good. Hopefully, she'll know something to help unravel this situation. I'll be right out." Selina closed the door to the small bathroom and stripped off her shirt. She had little time, but the most important thing was to check her incision and ensure there was no sign of infection. As she peeled back the bandage, the incision slowly revealed itself, and she couldn't help but grimace. She had seen it yesterday but hadn't been with it enough to consider the scope of the repair to her fascia. No wonder her entire abdomen was black and blue. The incision was jagged, leaving a zigzag down her skin with a puckered center where the entry wound was. She also had an exit wound when the bullet had left her body and slammed into the back of her vest. It took her a minute to realize she would have to rely on Efren to check that incision. The mirror didn't go low enough, and she couldn't twist around without pain to see it herself.

Her sigh was heavy, and he could probably hear it

out there, but there was little she could do other than re-dress the front incision and run a washcloth around her face and belly. After quickly brushing her teeth, she pulled her sweatshirt back on. "You've got this," she told the woman in the mirror. "It's just a Band-Aid. You can handle having his hands on you for that long."

The truth was, she couldn't handle having Efren's hands on her at all. Last night, when he held her hand and rubbed his thumb over it, she nearly fell apart on the spot. If she hadn't been so exhausted, she probably would have. It had been eight years since she'd encountered the intimate touch of a man who cared. That day, those few minutes of her life, had haunted her every day since then. Whenever she thought about Kai Tanner, her heart broke again. Vaccaro's venom poisoned more than just his victim. It traveled insidiously through their loved ones until they, too, suffered the wrath of the Snake.

Chapter Six

Eva watched and waited while the man she had known, and probably loved, finished the short climb up the bluff in the middle of nowhere, Wisconsin, and then bent over to catch his breath.

"I need your help, Kai."

His head snapped up when she stepped into the open, her dog Zeus standing steadfastly by her side. She saw the flare of love in his eyes. The same flare she'd seen for the last several years whenever they met up on a rescue. "I'll do anything I can, Eva."

"I have to run, Kai, and I'm going to need your help to get out of this alive." She spent the next few minutes outlining her plan.

"You want me to make a false report of your death?" Kai asked, taking a step back. "I doubt the authorities would appreciate that, Eva. If the ruse was uncovered, I could be charged."

"You won't be," she promised. "That's why I picked the bluffs. Falling into the river from up here is certain death, and a body would be washed away before a witness could even get to civilization for help. You're a search-and-rescue guy. If you tell them I never resurfaced, they'll

*believe you. They won't try hard to find me and assume
my body will wash ashore or end up in the Mississippi.
Eventually, they'll forget about me and move on with life."*

*"I'll never forget about you, Eva," Kai said, his head
shaking. "You've been the best partner a guy could have
in this business. I'll never work with someone like you
again. You lead with your moral compass, which is rare
these days. I don't want to do this." His lip trembled
when he put his hand on his hip in some form of defi-
ance she didn't understand.*

*"Never say never, Kai. You're the kind of guy who
attracts like-minded people. In my opinion, you're the
best of the best. I hope you understand now why I always stayed hands-off with you. I will always love you
even though I can never love you." She pressed Zeus's
leash into his palm. "Take him for me. Give him the life
I can't now."*

*"No," he said before she even finished. "No. You
aren't leaving, Eva. Stay. We can work this out."*

*"There are only two ways of working this out, Kai.
They both require me to die, fake or real. If I stay, the
Snake will be certain my death is real." Eva wished she
was wrong, but she wasn't. She'd crossed the wrong
man, and now, if she wanted to stay alive, she would
have to die.*

*"I'm not ready to say goodbye, Eva. There is so much
left unsaid."*

*"There's nothing you can do for me now, Kai," she
insisted. "Except to promise me you'll take care of Zeus
and give him a good life."*

*She could see the terror that filled him, but he finally
nodded. "And you're sure I won't get in trouble for this?"*

"Positive," Eva promised. "You have to know I don't have any other option. I wouldn't do this if I did."

"I know, but Eva, he's going to be heartbroken. I don't know if he'll ever recover."

"Zeus will be fine." She hoped someday Kai would be, too. "As long as he's got you and Apollo and can search, he'll find his purpose."

He choked back a sob and nodded. "We'll take care of him."

"I left his papers and money for his care in my truck at the entrance to the park. It should get you through quite a few years. I'm sorry I can't do more."

"No," he said, trailing a finger down her cheek. "Don't apologize for doing the right thing despite knowing the right thing meant a bounty on your head. I'll do my best to give him the kind of life and love you would have."

She knelt and wrapped her arms around the German shepherd's neck, whispering into his ear and stroking his fur. The pain in her chest was almost overwhelming. She'd lost her family to the Snake, and now he was taking the final things she loved.

Eva stood, and Kai grasped her elbow. "When it's safe, check my blog. I'll post updates about Zeus and Apollo as they work together. There will be pictures. It's the best I can do."

"Thank you," she said, raising up on her toes to kiss his cheek. "You are a genuinely good human, Kai. Find someone to love who's deserving of yours."

He grasped her hand. "You are deserving of love, Eva." He held tight to her hand as she tried to turn away. "I'll go with you. Let me grab Apollo."

"No." The one word was firm and heartbreaking.

"For this to work, I need you to play your part. The Snake will know I took off if you aren't here to run interference."

Kai nodded, and she noticed him blink back the tears that filled his eyes. "Okay, I've got your back."

She threw her arms around his neck and held him momentarily before doing the same to Zeus. "You know what to do?" she asked, standing again and holding his gaze.

"I'll set the scene. You get out of dodge. I love ya, partner. Be safe."

Eva blew him a kiss, turned and ran like the hounds of hell were after her.

"Selina?" Efren's voice snapped her from the daydream, and she gasped, the sound loud in the concrete room. "I'm coming in."

When he opened the door, their eyes locked, and before she had truly returned to the world, he pulled her from the bathroom and into his arms. Efren held her lightly, one arm wrapped around her back and one holding her head to his shoulder. She couldn't help but catalog everything about him in quick succession. His muscular chest was warm and tight. His cheek smelled like cedar soap and shaving cream as it rested against hers. His arm wrapped around her waist was soft and warm against her skin. It took her a moment to realize she hadn't pulled her shirt down all the way, and it was trapped above his arm, allowing his heat to pour into her. What settled in somewhere deep inside was the way he held her against him gently, and while careful of her wounds, he still made her feel safe in a world she knew wasn't.

"You look like you've seen a ghost," he murmured. "Are you in pain?"

"Not physically," she answered, her words rough to her own ears. "I was thinking about the last time I had to run from the Snake." Rather than go any further, she snapped her lips shut.

"I can't pretend to know what you're going through, Selina," Efren whispered, squeezing her a bit tighter. "Just know that we all have your back and we'll stop at nothing to protect you from Vaccaro."

"I know." The two words were whispered, but they held so many emotions. Fear. Gratefulness. Regret.

"We don't hold a grudge at Secure One." He'd turned his head so his lips brushed her ear when he spoke. The sensations rocketing through her made her want to collapse to the ground, and she would have, had he not been holding her. "Have you ever held it against any of them when their demons attacked you unexpectedly?"

"No."

"The same is true for you, Selina. We'll get through this, and the team will be stronger for it."

She lifted her head, prepared to pull away, but instead, she laid her lips on his. They were warm, moist and open, as though they'd been waiting for this moment their entire life. She couldn't help but notice how perfectly matched they were as his settled against hers for a hairbreadth before he leaned into the kiss. He caressed her lips, keeping it tender but barely contained until she forced herself to step back out of the hug and stand on her own.

She didn't want to. Lord, how she didn't want to, and that scared her, too. Efren was the enemy. You didn't kiss the enemy. Because of him, she had been overlooked and cast aside as an operative by Cal and the rest of the team. She was supposed to hate him, not find refuge in his arms and lips. Even if the game had changed and he was no longer her biggest enemy, she had to stay hands— and now lips—off. She couldn't help but notice the way his gaze raked her from head to toe and back up again to rest at her midsection, where her shirt still hung haphazardly, allowing her pink and puckered flesh to peek out. His gaze warmed her skin and insides, sending heat spiraling through her at an alarming speed. She had to put the brakes on whatever this was before things got out of control and she started to like the man in front of her. She already liked that kiss way too much.

"I—I need some help with the wound on my back." She had no idea how to address what happened, so her game plan was to pretend it didn't. "Will you check it and rebandage it? I can't reach it from any angle."

"Sure." The word was growled, and she couldn't help but notice that his hands were in fists as he walked to the bathroom for the first aid kit. "I'm glad you mentioned it, because I'd forgotten about the exit wound."

"I haven't," she said, tongue in cheek. "It's annoying to sleep on that bandage. I'm hoping we can cover it with a regular Band-Aid at this point."

He swung a chair around and had her sit on the edge so he had a clear view of her back. After the supplies were readied on the table, he started working the bandage off her skin a little at a time. "The team is ready as soon as we are," he said, giving her something else to focus on as he worked. "They're anxious to put eyes on you so they can see that you're okay."

"I'm worried they're angry," she admitted. The truth was easier to speak when not staring directly into his eyes.

"That's one thing you don't have to worry about." He dabbed liquid around the wound. It stung for just a moment, but then cool air stole it away, telling her he was fanning her skin to avoid hurting her. "From what I can gather, Cal knew the truth?"

"Some of it, but not the full scope. He was going to run a background check on me, and there was no way that was going to work. He had a…reputation, so I leaned into that in hopes he'd understand."

"As the kind of guy you could trust with your secrets because he had a mountain of his own?"

"Bingo." She hissed as he probed the edges of the wound. "What are you doing?"

"Sorry," he said, popping his head around her shoulder. "It's a little pink, but your reaction said it's pink from healing and not infection."

"Take a picture of it," she said, waiting for him to grab the Secure One phone. He handed it around to her, and she inspected it closely, trying not to visibly grimace at how ugly it was. "Well, I've taken better pictures. Let's put some antibiotic ointment around the edges just to be on the safe side, but avoid the stitches."

He squeezed her shoulder. "You're alive. Remember that and use it to fight through this. Someone else tried to take you down, but you stood tall. That mark on your skin is a badge of honor."

"Change the narrative and change the world, right?"

"Not the world," he disagreed, as he swiped ointment around the wound and grabbed a large bandage from the pack. "Just your mindset. I already know you're a fighter,

Selina, so keep fighting. Don't let a Loraine bullet be the bullet that takes you down, physically or emotionally. They don't deserve to hold that kind of power over you. That much you know for sure." He pulled her shirt down over the wound and patted her back. "You're good to go."

Selina stood and stretched her back before giving a nod. "Thanks. It feels better to get that big bandage off there."

"Happy to do it." He threw away the old bandages and cleaned up the first aid kit before he washed his hands.

"Brenna," she said, and he turned, drying his hands on a towel. "I appreciate the pep talk. I got caught up in the past and you helped me refocus."

"Understandable," he said, tipping his head to the side. "It happens to all of us, which is what I like about working at Secure One. There's always someone there who understands and can pull you back before that rabbit hole goes too deep."

"Speaking of Secure One, I suppose we should make that call."

"Deep breath," he said, walking toward her until he was standing chest to chest with her again. She followed his order, and they took a deep breath together and let it out. "Good. You didn't even grimace with that breath. You must be feeling better," he said with a wink.

"I'm glad for it, too. The less medication I have to take, the sharper my mind will be."

"That's true, but you also have to be able to move quickly with little or no notice."

Selina tipped her head back and forth. "I'll take over-the-counter painkillers, but keep the other ones on me. I can always pop one fast if we have to go. That said,

I'd give anyone major props who can find the entrance to this place. Cal didn't even tell the team where it was or how to find it."

"He wanted it need-to-know, so I didn't find out until last night when he sent the location to my GPS."

"That's Cal for you. The fewer people who know, the better. Time to make that call," she finally said, settling herself down at the computer terminal. He sat next to her and leaned into her ear.

"You can pretend that kiss never happened, but it did, and I'm not going to pretend that I didn't feel the connection between us. Fair warning."

His piece said, he clicked a button on a device next to him without another word.

Chapter Seven

Efren's words replayed on repeat in her mind. "Fair warning." Was he implying that he planned to kiss her again? The very idea made her nervous. Not because she didn't want him to, but because she did. Getting involved with anyone could mean instant death for them. If necessary, she'd remind herself of that every second of the day. She couldn't be the reason an innocent person died at Vaccaro's hands.

Before she could speak, a familiar voice filled their concrete prison. "Secure one, Charlie."

"Secure two, Tango," Efren responded, and the screen flickered to life.

"Secure three, Sierra," she finished, and Cal's face filled the screen.

"You're a sight for sore eyes," he said without preamble. "How are you feeling?"

"Better. I've had worse injuries."

"Maybe, but our goal now is to get you through this without more." Cal set his jaw for a moment and then shook his head. "I'm going to flip the camera."

Selina nodded, and they waited until the conference room came into view. Mina, Roman, Mack, Eric, Lucas,

Cal, Charlotte and Marlise sat around the table. That was their core team, and Cal couldn't make it clearer he was sticking with them to get this job done. Awkward wasn't Selina's style, but staring into the faces of the people she'd lied to for years was exactly that. So much so that she didn't know what to say.

"We're a team," Eric said, standing and leaning on the table with his hands to peer into the camera. "We've been a team for years, and that doesn't change now. Is that understood, Sierra?"

Her nod was instant and quick. "Heard and understood, Echo."

Eric sat with a nod.

Mina spoke next. "Good to see you, Selina. We've been getting updates from Efren, but it's not the same as talking to you. Before we go any further, we all want to know the answer to one question." She motioned around the circle of people, so Selina nodded for her to ask it. "Going forward, do you want to go by Eva or Selina?"

"Selina." There was no hesitation in her answer. "Eva Shannon is dead. Do you all understand? She must remain dead and buried for more reasons than I have time to go into right now."

"He already knows you're alive," Marlise said. "No matter what name you go by, the bounty is on your head."

"I understand that, but if I'm going to get through this and figure out how Ava Shannon came back from the dead and why, I need distance. The only way to separate myself from my twin is to pretend I am someone else entirely."

"You are," Efren said, slipping his arm around her

back where no one else could see. "You may be twins genetically, but not in morals or anything else that matters."

"He's right," Cal said with a nod. "That's the reason I hired you eight years ago with the weak story that you were a domestic violence victim on the run. That's also the reason we've got your back today even knowing that story you sold was fiction." All the heads around the table nodded as he spoke, and it lifted her tired lips into a smile.

"Thanks, team. My greatest fear was my attitude over the last few months damaged our relationship and you wouldn't want to work with me."

"Never," Mack said before anyone else could speak. "We all have our own brand of attitude depending on the day and situation. That's accepted within this circle, as you well know. You've been on the receiving end of my attitude more often than not."

"I still feel bad about it," she said, biting her lip.

"That's because you're a good person in your heart, and you don't want to hurt people," Charlotte said. "You got me through those first few days after I turned myself in and I was too scared to speak. It was you who kept me calm and made me feel safe even when I wasn't. Let us do that for you now."

A breath escaped her chest as though she'd been punched. "Thank you, Charlotte. I needed to hear you say that. It shifted my guilt and brought the reason we're here into focus. Getting out of this alive."

"It was the least I could do," Charlotte assured her.

Cal drummed his fingers on the table, and all heads turned to him. It was magical how he made those metal and plastic fingers behave just like real ones. "It's time for full disclosure, Colvert. The moment someone said the Loraine name a few weeks ago you should have been in my office, but we can't go backward, so let's go forward. Tell us why you're in their crosshairs."

She took a deep breath, knowing she had to bare her soul if they were going to save it. Efren rubbed her hip, his warm hand what she needed to ground her in order to tell the sordid tale again. She did it with as little emotion as possible as she filled them in on her family's involvement with the Mafia and her crossing of them during her law enforcement career.

"You're saying your sister didn't die that night?" Roman asked when she finished telling them about the raid.

"That appears to be the case, since she showed up at the hospital asking for me."

Eric shook his head and chuckled. "When I told the charge nurse to watch for someone suspicious asking about you, I never dreamed that person would look exactly like you. I was expecting a hit man."

"Trust me, Eric, she was the hit man. If Efren hadn't gotten me out of there, you'd be attending my real funeral right now. My twin believes in the whole Mafia mentality of an eye for an eye, and when that eye is family, she will stop at nothing to make you pay. What I don't know is why she's not dead and how she knew I wasn't either."

"I've got some feelers out in regard to the Loraine family. Unfortunately, I don't have any answers," Mina interjected.

"Yet," Roman added with a wink.

"I've concentrated my efforts on Randall Loraine Sr.,"

she explained, clicking a slide up onto the screen for them to see. "As you know, he's resided at Federal Correctional Institution Pekin for the last eight years serving a fifty-year sentence for the counterfeiting scheme. Since he was convicted of a nonviolent crime, he is in a low-security institution."

Selina rolled her eyes. "The crime may have been nonviolent, but trust me, Randall Sr. knows how to be violent."

"I have no doubt of that, considering who he worked for," Mina agreed. "From what I can see of his records, he hasn't had any visitors since Howie Loraine was last there to see him shortly before his death almost a month ago. However, prior to that, Howie visited him once every two weeks for the entire time he's been there. Randall Jr. visited him once a month without fail."

"So maybe Howie and Randall were continuing Daddy's business on the outside?"

"More than likely," Eric agreed. "But we already suspected that was the case."

"None of that explains how my twin came back to life." Selina heard the frustration in her voice and tried to curb it. This wasn't her friends' fault, and she needed their help if she was going to come out of this bunker alive.

"I'm working on that as well," Mina promised. "I've pulled the information from that night, and I'm following the chain of people who were in contact with your sister from the time you shot her until she was pronounced 'dead.'" She used air quotes around the word, considering the circumstances. "My hope is to follow the money. If any of them got a large influx of cash, I'll find it."

Selina leaned forward, partly to free herself of Efren's warm hand on her side and partly to be seen better, so no one misunderstood what she was saying. "If Ava didn't die eight years ago, there's a connection somewhere between her and Vaccaro. We need to find that connection and follow where it leads."

"That's easier said than done," Mina answered. "The Vaccaro organization is one organization I can't hack. I can use back channels to find out what the organization is doing, but anything personal is off-limits to me."

"The Snake doesn't allow anyone into his den who he doesn't invite in as a warm body or a meal." Selina shivered involuntarily. "Is there a way to find out who Randall Jr. talked to the night he was arrested?"

"Like, did he make any phone calls?" Mina asked, her hands poised over the keyboard.

"Or have any visitors," Selina said. "I wonder if Randall Jr. knew she wasn't dead since he hung out so much with his father in prison. If he did, he may have been the one to report to her or Vaccaro that I was alive."

"He knew it was you since he already knew that Ava was alive and where she was," Efren finished, nodding immediately.

Eric spoke up. "Honestly, Eva and Ava are impossible to tell the difference when lip reading. It was dark and we were all moving. Randall Jr. could have said Eva and I wouldn't know. That would explain why he shot you."

"There was a lot of law enforcement there that night. If one of them was a plant by Vaccaro, they could have reported back that they saw Selina," Roman suggested.

"Since Randall Jr. already knew Ava was alive, he knew it was me." Selina clenched her jaw in frustration.

"We're assuming that Randall, and thus Vaccaro, knew Ava was still alive," Cal said, holding up a finger. "Until we know that for sure, we can't assume anything."

"Easiest way to find out is to start with Randall Jr. I can hopefully have an answer in a few hours," Mina said without taking her hands off the keyboard.

Selina smiled at her friend and nodded. "I know it won't be easy, but until we know why she's back, our hands are tied. That said, I assure you that Vaccaro is aware that Ava is still alive. I would go so far as to say he's the *reason* she's still alive."

"You think she's been working in his organization all these years?" Mack asked.

Selina's nod was exaggerated. "Without a doubt."

Cal waved his hand in the air. "What I don't get is, why Vaccaro was building an organization outside of his family. Our basic understanding of him says he's over the age of sixty. Shouldn't his children be the ones layered up into his organization? Isn't that how the Mafia works?"

"You're correct." Selina pointed at the screen with a smile. "Here's where things get interesting. Vaccaro is the last of his line. His swimmers didn't swim if you catch my drift?" Heads nodded around the table. "Since he never had children, he made his wife his second-in-command. A queenpin if you will. She was ten years younger than him, but she died of cancer about ten years ago. I have no idea what's transpired since, whether he's remarried or not, but that's beside the point. There are no children, so his only choice was to find other families he could corrupt and pull in to build his organization."

"It seems that his choices were a bit off?" Roman asked.

"In hindsight," Selina agreed. "My father and Randall Sr. were his buddies from college, so it made sense for him to pull them in. He trusted them to have children and raise them to be part of the business. He forgot that children live what they learn, and corruption doesn't always swing in your favor when the chips are down."

"He also forgot that some are simply not corruptible," Efren said, giving her a gentle shoulder bump. "All of that said, it's time for us to get back to Secure One."

"No." Selina's objection was loud and precise when she stood on the two letters.

"Selina, we're safer behind the layers of security at home than we'll ever be anywhere else."

"Maybe," she said, spinning to stick her finger in his chest. He stood, which made her smile inside. He was not going to be the beta male in this game if he could help it. "But I won't risk opening Secure One to the Vaccaro organization. That would be certain death for every single person sitting around that table. Is that what you want?"

"You're overreacting." She noticed him grit his teeth and make a fist before he spoke again. "We can't stay here. We have to move, and the most logical place is back to Secure One."

"I disagree with you, Tango," Cal said from the head of the table. "We already put Secure One at risk by going into the Loraine mansion to get Kadie and Vic. It was the right thing to do, but it opened us up to an attack that even our security measures may not be able to withstand. All I can do is hope they're too busy scrambling to get Randall Jr. out of jail and find Selina to worry about what we are doing. The last thing I want is for them to get wind that Selina is here."

"To that end," Marlise said, "I've made you disappear. Your credit card was used to buy a ticket to Hawaii and you were seen getting on the plane with a male resembling Efren."

"I doubt that will buy us much time," Selina said. "Thanks for trying, though."

"That one may not," Cal said, wearing a smirk. "The other five will probably slow them down, though."

"You bought six different plane tickets?" Efren asked, laughter bubbling out of him. "That's diabolical level stuff."

"This is life-or-death level stuff," Cal said. "I know Vaccaro won't believe you're on one flight, but if he's suddenly faced with six, he has no choice but to check them out, just in case. My goal is to keep the heat off you long enough to get some healing time in and to buy me time to find you somewhere else to go. When I built that bunker, I didn't have hiding an operative from the Mafia on my bingo card."

"That's my fault, I know," Selina agreed. "I can tell you until I'm blue in the face how bad I feel about that, but I'd rather get through this alive so I can make it up to you on the next case."

"There's the spirit!" Mina exclaimed, giving her an air high five. "Hang tight there and get some rest. Let us work on things on our end and before you know it, you'll be back in your lab doing your thing."

Efren looked like he was about to object when Cal spoke. "I'll contact you on the secure line if I need you to call in. While you wait, rest, and if you think of anything more to help us find your sist—" He held his hand up. "I'm sorry, find Ava Shannon, let me know immediately. We'll be in touch again at 2100 hours for an update. If you have to move before that, you know the drill."

Efren gave him a salute right before the screen went dark. Selina paced to the other end of the bunker in silence. "The Snake will know it's a ruse." The words were muttered rather than spoken. "He won't take the bait. He'll know I'm still here. We have to move."

"No." Efren grasped her arms and held her in place. "We have nowhere to go."

"We can't stay here." She looked up into his eyes and wondered if hers told a louder story than her words. "He will find us and he will kill us!" Before she could say another word, his lips were on hers.

Chapter Eight

Stop kissing her. Efren's inner voice demanded he listen, but he wasn't. He dug in deeper, drawing her into him with a hand at her waist and his other hand buried deep in her long, silky hair. She was butter under his lips and sagged against him as they stood in the silent room. She poured her pain, anger, fear and guilt into him, and he willingly swallowed it all. He'd been with plenty of women over the years, but none of them could bring him to his knees with a kiss the way Selina did. And she would always be Selina to him. He would fight for her and with her until his dying breath, if need be, but he'd rather make love, not war. That was all he was thinking about as his lips stroked hers. Selina slid her arms around his waist and moaned softly, telling him she was as into it as he was, despite the danger they faced from Vaccaro and what getting personally involved might bring down on them.

Too damn bad.

"We have to stop," she murmured against his lips before pulling away. "We can't let this distract us and leave ourselves open to an attack."

"You're right." The words were as heavy as the breath in his chest. "I just can't deny this spark between us any longer. We've fought against it for months, but this was inevitable."

"Was it though?" she asked as she walked to the bed and sat. "I'm still mad at you. Don't think for a minute that I've forgotten how you became part of the team at Secure One."

"What does that mean, Selina?"

"I can't do this right now, Brenna. I need to rest." She'd scooted under the blankets and closed her eyes by the time he approached the bunks.

"It's interesting how you call me by my last name as soon as I get a little too close or you feel a little too vulnerable. Sleep now, but know there will come a day where we'll work out this grudge you've got against me. The way you kiss me tells me it will be worth it."

He waited, but she never responded, just kept on with her fake sleep. He'd allow it, for now, but he'd spoken the truth. One day, they'd have it out and once the air was cleared, he had every intention of exploring this heat between them. For now, he had to do what he could to get them out of this bind. To do that, he'd have to understand the enemy.

Efren waited for Selina's breathing to even out so he knew she was actually sleeping and then grabbed the Secure One phone. He typed out a message to Mina, whose response came within minutes. Sure thing. While Selina slept, he intended to learn everything he could about Vaccaro and the Shannons. Not so much about Eva as much as Ava. He would have to have a handle on what her sister was capable of if he was going to stay one step ahead of them. If that was even possible. If Vaccaro was half as powerful as they said he was—and he had no reason to doubt them—then his only choice might be to go stealth mode and literally stay one step ahead of them until the team could figure out how to bring them in.

He grabbed a bottle of water and a package of trail mix, then fired up the direct link computer. He'd have to wait until the satellite passed over to get the transmission, but with any luck, the info Mina was sending would be what he needed to get to not only know the enemy but better understand the woman he one day wanted in his bed. That truth hit him in the gut. If they somehow managed to cut off the head of this snake, he'd stop at nothing to prove to Selina that letting go of her anger and making room for him in her life was worth the risk.

He glanced at her and couldn't help but smile. That may be easier said than done, but he was up for the challenge.

SELINA WOKE SLOWLY, her head pounding and her belly sore when she sat up. "Oh Lord, end me." The words were grunted in pain. Efren was beside her almost instantly, helping her stand.

"I'll do no such thing, but I think you may have hit the seventy-two-hour hell."

"I couldn't agree more." She couldn't stand up straight, so she just sat back down. The seventy-two-hour hell was a place no one wanted to be after surgery. It was always the third day that everything hit you like a ton of bricks. The pain, fatigue the healing, and for her the fear, combined to make the next few hours miserable until she got everything under control again.

"Take this," Efren said, handing her a pill, but she pushed it away. "Take it. This is not up for argument."

He held out a bottle of water and she grudgingly took the pill and forced herself to drink most of the water.

"I can't keep taking the heavy stuff," she said, leaning over on her thighs. "I have to shake this pain off and get ready for battle."

"Not treating your pain is going to make that impossible," he said, pulling the chair over to sit across from her. "You had a bullet in your belly, and it did some funky stuff to your body. Acknowledge that and accept it, so we can stop having this same argument every time you wake up."

"Why did I get trapped in a bunker with a smart-ass?" Her words were tongue-in-cheek, but she also meant them.

"More like a badass," he answered with a wink. "A badass who made you more soup and crackers and wants you to feel better because he knows how miserable you are right now. Speaking in generalities of course, since my last surgery wasn't gut surgery."

"What was your last surgery?" He helped her up and walked with her to the table where she sat again and waited for him to bring her the soup that he'd been heating up for her. He knew when she woke up, she was going to need food.

"Limb revision." He set a bowl in front of her with rice and chicken in broth. "That was about six years ago."

"How long ago was the original amputation?"

"Ten. They originally left my knee, but that limited my options for prosthetics, so I opted to go above the knee when the original amputation had to be revised anyway."

"They should have gone above the knee to start, right?"

"It would have saved me a lot of headaches, but traumatic amputations, as you know, are tricky. They did the best they could, and I was functional with a through the knee, but I'm outstanding above the knee." He winked to tell her he was joking, but she shook her head.

"You actually are outstanding above the knee. Considering what you've been through, you've come back from it well. I just wish you gave your limb more time to rest. I never see you without the prosthesis. Do you sleep with it?"

"No." He lowered himself to the chair across from her. "After the revision, I developed strong phantom pain. With the original injury, it was there, but it was more a minor annoyance in the background. This is not that. It's mind numbing and distracting, and the only way I found to deal with it is to keep compression on the limb at all times. It feels good in the socket, so at night, I have a soft one I wear to help with the pain while I sleep. The medication I take helps as well."

"Do you have your meds with you?" She asked the question with the spoon halfway to her mouth and a brow raised. Once the question was out, she finished spooning in the soup while keeping a close eye on him. She would know if he was lying.

"Some."

"Not enough, right?"

"Not for an extended period, no. I'm rationing them for now."

"And if you run out?"

"Not an option, so if we can't get back to Secure One,

Cal may have to make an unexpected airdrop. We'll cross that bridge when we come to it."

"I want to say it won't come to it, but I am all too familiar with this game. We aren't going back to Secure One anytime soon."

"After what I read, I have to agree." He tapped his fingers on the table. "I knew from the moment I met you that you were someone special, but all of this leaves me speechless."

"All of what? My hot mess express?"

"No, that you willingly took on a kingpin knowing you were signing your own death warrant. There aren't many people in the world who would do that."

"They would if they'd seen what I had in life." Her shrug at the end probably told him more than her words, but she couldn't worry about that now. Her secrets were no longer secrets, but she still wasn't comfortable with him knowing even the little bit she'd told him.

"I spent the night reading through the articles Mina sent me, and I stand by my statement. Not many people would do what you did."

"Articles?" Selina laid her spoon down, the soup threatening to come back up at the idea that he had information outside of what she'd given him. If she couldn't control the narrative, then she had no control left whatsoever. For someone like her, that was more terrifying than facing off with a kingpin.

"Mina dug through the archives and found some old articles about the Snake. His moniker is fitting."

She exhaled a bit at his words. Old articles on the Snake were okay. Old articles about her would leave her open to more questions than she wanted to answer.

She was no longer the woman who fell off that cliff eight years ago. He couldn't get that idea in his head or it would be too hard for him to consider her an equal going forward.

"I thought I had a lot of medals. Then I read your bio."

Selina's heart sank. "I don't know what you mean. I don't have any medals."

"Not what I read. Sounds like you were not only a decorated Chicago PD cop, but you were an up-and-comer in the search-and-rescue world as well. Did you know they awarded you the valor award posthumously?"

Selina stood, no longer caring about the pain in her belly. The pain in her chest overpowered it. She wanted out of this bunker and away from Efren Brenna. She'd gotten used to hiding out in the lab at Secure One to avoid him and his damn tempting eyes, but here, there was nowhere to go, and she suspected he was taking full advantage of the situation. He liked making her uncomfortable. It was probably something they taught them in the military, like, live on the edge of your comfort zone, and soon you'll be comfortable in all the zones. She snorted at herself and offered herself a mental high five for that gem.

What was she supposed to say? No, she had no idea they bestowed upon her the most respected award in law enforcement after she faked her death.

"It's okay, you know," he said from directly behind her. "They didn't award it to you because you died. They awarded it to you because you lived."

Her shoulders sank, and he wrapped his arms around them, holding her against his chest. Every time they touched, his settled her somewhere deep inside that even

she couldn't pinpoint. Or maybe she didn't want to pinpoint it and admit that his touch had power over her.

"Maybe I lived honestly, but I died dishonestly. I bet
they wouldn't have considered that so medal-worthy."

"It's no different than going into WITSEC and falling off the face of the earth. The difference is, when you
go into WITSEC, you don't get to shape the narrative.
At least you did it your way. You did it in a way that reminded people, sometimes the heroes that go out to save
them don't always come back."

Selina grabbed his forearms and held on tight, letting
his heat warm and relax her. "I suppose that's true, but
some might call what I did taking the coward's way out."

"Anyone who thinks that hasn't read the articles I
have on Medardo Vaccaro. You took the only out you had
at the time. Never consider your contributions to taking
that man down as less than because of the choices you
had to make after the attempt. You had no good ones, so
you took the one that hurt the fewest number of people."

"How do you figure?" She was curious to know why
he thought that was the best choice she could have made.

"Listen, you're talking to someone who ran a lot of
missions in a lot of hostile places. Our first instruction
if we were caught was to take any opportunity to end
our lives before they could get information from us.
The movies make it look like you can escape any situation when captured in a war or hostile territory, but the
truth is, no one escapes. The enemy gets the information
from you in the most painful way possible, and then you
die. Make no mistake. You were in a war with no team
and no one willing to protect you from the enemy. You
already knew the police department suspected you of

being involved with the Snake. They weren't likely to bend over backward to protect you from him, right?"

"If I'd thought it was likely, I wouldn't have run."

"Then you did what soldiers do. Sure, you didn't die, but you've spent the years since you disappeared doing good for other people. You've continued to rescue those in need, even if the way you do it looks a little bit different."

Selina said nothing, she just leaned her head back and let the words he said settle deep inside her where she could call them up whenever she doubted the decisions she'd made over the years. There was one important thing she had to do before they spent any more time togeth—

"Secure one, Whiskey."

Efren dropped his arms and hurried to the console with Selina on his heels. "Secure two, Tango."

Mina's face popped up on the screen, and she eyed them both. "I have an update, and you may want to sit down for this."

Chapter Nine

Efren's gaze darted to Selina for a moment, and then he pulled out a chair, motioning for her to sit, which she did without argument. Whether it was fatigue from the surgery or opening up to him over the last few days that made her feel weak, he didn't know, but whatever Mina had to say was sure to change the game again.

"How bad is it?" Selina asked, her shoulders stiff as though she was preparing for battle.

"You'll have to answer that question. I learned through some back channels that Randall Sr. could be released on a technicality."

Silence. Efren counted to ten before he slid into the chair next to Selina and hooked his arm around her waist. He didn't care if Mina saw him do it, either. He could see in Selina's eyes that her world was spinning and she needed someone to ground her. While he couldn't be everything for her, as the only one here, he could support her.

"Do you know why he's being released?" Efren asked since Selina had opened her mouth, but only a puff of air escaped.

"I'm working on learning that and what his release date will be."

"That explains why Ava is back now." Selina said her sister's name as though it were venom on her tongue she had to spit out. "Still doesn't explain where she's been all these years."

"Working on that, too," Mina answered. "But if she's within the Vaccaro organization, I won't find much."

"I have no doubt she is," Selina said with conviction. "Did you get anywhere with Randall Jr.'s arrest?"

"I have a few feelers out. The information is fresh, so it will take a bit longer to get."

"Understood," Efren said. "Thanks for the update. At least we know why Ava has shown her face again."

"Ever the loving wife. Give me a break," Selina muttered. "Are you sure there were no unnamed visitors visiting Daddy Dearest in prison?"

Mina smiled the smile she wore when she was a dog with a bone. "Great minds think alike. I broke down his visitor list, and I'm looking into the names individually. If she was there, I'll find out."

"Thanks, Mina—"

Before he could say more, Cal loomed over Mina's shoulder. "My surveillance indicates our attempts to throw off anyone looking for Selina has failed. Someone has been sniffing around the Jeep, and I haven't been able to get it out of there. Stay on your toes."

"I've always got an eye on the trail cameras," he assured his boss. Did he feel guilty for lying since he spent half his time staring at Selina? Not even a little bit.

"Good. We'll be in touch as soon as we know Randall's court date and the technicality."

"Selina," Mina said before Cal could end the transmission. "Would Vaccaro put out a hit on you, or do you think this is purely Ava's axe to grind?"

Selina was silent longer than necessary to think about the question, which told Efren she was hiding something. "If the Snake knows I'm alive, he would want me as dead as Ava does, so a hit would be pointless. He'd send my twin after me."

Mina turned and smiled at Cal. "Told ya."

When she turned back, she winked at Selina.

"You're saying the real person we need to track is Ava?" Cal asked, and this time, Selina nodded immediately.

"I have no question. Ava has her own agenda, but this time, it lines up with the Snake's, so he's probably given her his blessing to take me out by any means necessary."

"All because you were a cop?" Efren asked.

"If you cross Vaccaro, no matter how small, you will pay. I knew that going in, but I held on to hope that if we could bust Randall and Ava for counterfeiting, that trail would lead us to Vaccaro and we could finally arrest him."

"You don't know if that happened, right?" Mina asked.

"If they found evidence leading to Vaccaro?" she asked, and Mina nodded. "If we know he's not in prison, then they didn't find anything. I assume since Randall was tried and sent to prison, the police were able to prove he was running the ring."

"There's nothing you can think of offhand that would be a reason they'd be releasing Randall now?"

"No," Selina said. "This is so frustrating!" Her fist hit the table and bounced until Efren grabbed it and held it between his hands.

"Take a deep breath." His whisper calmed her immediately, and she inhaled and then exhaled.

"Sorry." She glanced up at Mina and Cal, still on the screen. "It's hard to be here and not there. It's like watching someone save your life, but you aren't a participant in it."

"You very much are, though," Cal said to reassure her. "Your job is to keep your wits about you there and to answer our questions as information comes in. I know it feels like you aren't doing anything, but hang in there. We've all got your back, and the one who has your physical back is the best in the business. If he says jump, you don't ask questions, got it?"

Selina gave him a salute, and Mina promised to be in touch soon before they signed off.

"I can't believe they're releasing that lying sack of human flesh," she said in a sudden gush of fury and vitriol. "I gave up my life for this, and now he's going to walk free again!"

Efren was still holding her hand, and he massaged it until she relaxed the fist and let him caress her palm. "We don't know that yet. Don't jump to conclusions."

"What other conclusion can there be?" she demanded.

"It could be a retrial situation or house arrest. Let's give Mina a bit more time."

"Time, time." She muttered the words as she stood and paced the room. "We have so much time and never enough time. We're trapped here with nothing but time that we're wasting doing nothing to help them."

"We can't help them." Efren grasped her waist and held her in place. "But we aren't wasting time. We're biding our time. There is a difference. You need to heal and once I think you're ready, we'll leave this place and spend our time clearing your name."

Selina stared him down for the longest time before she spoke. "First off, I'm the medical professional here, not you. Second, there is no clearing my name. I'm either alive, and Ava is dead, or I'm dead and Ava is alive. Those are the only two outcomes."

"As a forever optimist, I believe there's a third option and that is you're alive and Ava is in prison next to her husband and the monster who is pulling her strings. We can do that at Secure One if we work together."

She reached up and patted his face, letting her fingers linger as they trailed away from his skin. His cheek heated from her touch, and he forced himself to stay focused on calming her enough to sleep. There would be time to explore this connection between them when her life wasn't on the line. He feared if he didn't convince her to rest, he'd use the time in this bunker unwisely, and that would cloud his decision-making process going forward.

"You're so innocent in the ways of the Mafia. I wish you could stay that way, but by the time this is over, you'll see the only proper place for these people is ten feet under. There is evil in this world that can't be reformed, and Vaccaro is the captain of that bus."

"You're saying the movies got it all wrong?" His words were light as he walked her backward toward the bed.

"There have been a handful of movies I could relate to as someone who grew up on the fringes of that lifestyle. Understanding the Mafia is impossible unless you live it, which I don't recommend. Unfortunately for you, you're about to live it."

"Don't feel bad for me, Selina Colvert." His words

were an order, and her eyes widened a touch as he lowered her to the bed. "I've taken out a lot of that evil you speak of. Mafia of a different kind, you could say. If I had guilt about it, that ended when I found scores of villagers dead with their tongues cut out. Those are the images I'll never unsee, but I don't lose any sleep at night over the men who I made sure never walked this earth again. I'm not afraid of doing the same thing to Vaccaro if it comes down to you or him. Understand?"

He waited for her to get comfortable, but she didn't—she pulled him down onto the bed next to her. "You're going to war for me?"

"Yes. Only because I want to, Selina." Efren turned and cradled her face in his hands. "Not because I have to."

"I'm sorry," she whispered, her hands grasping his wrists.

"For what, darling?"

"Asking you to wade into another war you didn't ask to fight."

His smile was gentle when he ran his thumbs across her lips. "You didn't ask. I offered. Those other wars I fought, they were faces I didn't see or know. This war... Well, this war has a name and a face of someone I care about, so I'm standing in front of you now asking for a gun and a chance to march beside you. Together we can end this war swiftly. First, you need some rest." His thumbs stroked her temples as her eyes drooped, despite how she fought to keep them open.

He leaned in and placed a gentle kiss on her lips. "Sleep now, my beauty. That is time not wasted while you heal your body."

"Lie with me," she murmured as he lowered her head to the pillow. "I don't want to be alone."

Before she finished the sentence he'd scooted her to the back of the bed, kicked off his shoe and lain next to her. After arranging his prosthesis so it didn't hurt her, he pulled her against him tightly and gently splayed his hand across her belly.

"Sleep now. Clear your mind and let it rest, too. I've got your back."

Selina may have drifted off to sleep, but that was the very last thing on Efren's mind. The thought of losing the woman in his arms to an animal like Loraine or Vaccaro filled his mind. He was trained to hunt animals hiding in a hole, smoke them out and then end their lives. He vowed he'd do the same thing with Vaccaro so Selina could have her life back, even if he had to sacrifice himself to do it.

An hour later, as he peeled himself away from her and walked to the cabinet where the go bags waited, he refused to look too deeply at why he was willing to sacrifice himself for a woman who had treated him with nothing but animosity since the day they'd met. Maybe it had something to do with the look in her eye when she did it, or maybe it had something to do with the way she touched him when her guard was down, but whatever the reason, when this job was over, he'd have to leave Secure One if he wanted solidarity again. A team was great, until someone got too close and opened you up to emotions you didn't know how to deal with after what you'd been through.

Death and destruction were the emotions he understood now. The soft caress of a woman desperate for a connection as her world spun out of control was something else entirely. The first one he could prepare and plan for. The second could only lead to one thing, and he'd already had enough heartbreak in his life to add more.

The touch of a woman was okay when it was no strings attached and no expectations, but it could never be that with Selina, and he knew it. The cost of being a hero was one he'd paid dearly for over the years. He may have saved six men that day, but only three of them remained all these years later. The scars of war went deep, and he was not immune to them just because he'd been the one doing the saving. What he learned was, you could rescue someone, but it was up to them to save themselves. Some could and some couldn't, but that wasn't his job. His job was to rescue or protect and then walk away, and that was exactly what he'd do again, even if it broke him to say goodbye to the brotherhood he'd found at Secure One.

He glanced behind him at the woman he considered part of that brotherhood, even if no one else on the team acknowledged the contributions she'd made to the business at a significant cost to her soul. That was the part that scared him the most. He understood that she suffered in silence out of some misplaced idea that stoicism was required to be part of the club. To be part of the inner circle that allowed you to do more than fix battle wounds and babysit. What surprised him the most was how angry it made him that she had to. He wasn't supposed to care. He wasn't supposed to get angry. He was supposed to do his job and move on to the next one. For the life of him, he couldn't figure out when that had changed. That was a lie. He knew the exact moment it changed, but he couldn't, and didn't want to, give it space in his head.

Efren turned away from Selina with determination. Once they made it through this battle, he was done pretending that protecting people would bring back those he'd already lost. It was time for a new path, and no matter how much he wished it were different, that path would not include Selina Colvert.

Chapter Ten

Selina woke with a start, immediately registering that all the lights were low. On guard, she sat up and searched the room until her gaze landed on Efren's back. He stood at the consoles in deep concentration.

"There are tactical clothes at the end of the bed. Get dressed in place. I'm not looking."

"Do we have a problem?"

"Potentially." His words were clipped and quiet. "Someone is sniffing around topside."

Selina stripped off her sweats and pulled on the black ripstop pants. They were a little big, but they'd have to do for now. She strapped on a belt that came complete with a holster and 9mm. After she adjusted them to protect the incisions on her front and back, she stripped off her sweatshirt, pulled on the black T-shirt and covered it with the sweatshirt, and then a lightweight black coat. She eyed the boots and before she could decide on a way to put them on, Efren was kneeling in front of her, tying on the boots for her.

"I can put on my own boots."

"I'd rather you save the energy for what's ahead of us. Grab your pills and take one. Just in case."

"I'm fine." She stood and stretched side to side to

prove it. "We've been here for a week now and it's nothing more than a slight twinge." His disapproving glance made her sigh, so she took two over-the-counter painkillers to satisfy him. "What are we dealing with here, Efren?"

They hadn't gotten an update from Mina since yesterday afternoon, which meant she wasn't breaking through any of Vaccaro's firewalls put up to keep her out, and keeping Mina Jacobs out was no easy feat.

"My eyes in the sky are showing me that the guys who found the Jeep didn't give up there. They've been poking around in the woods, too."

"Damn it. Have you let Secure One know?"

"Not yet. I'm not sure that they'll hang around if they don't find anything." He pointed at the camera where two groups of two guys moved through the woods, silent as ninjas. They wore night-vision goggles and carried big guns.

"How far out are they? Are we safe in here?"

"For now," he answered, his gaze still on the console. "They won't find our hatch in the dark if they don't know where it is. The daytime is a different story."

"You're saying we won't be here if they make it that far."

"Not if I have anything to say about it. Our go bags are packed. I made a small one for you to carry. It has the first aid kit and the little bit of tech we can take with us. I don't want you carrying anything heavier than that until we see how you do."

"Do you have a destination in mind?"

He turned and took her in, his gaze dark, intense and focused. "Somewhere that isn't here."

"Secure one, Whiskey."

Efren put his finger to his lips and then turned and answered the console quietly. "Secure two, Tango. Hush mode."

Selina waited until Mina's face popped up on the screen. She spoke, but it was impossible to hear what she was saying; all she could do was read the captions on the screen. Her first questions were, "Are you in danger? Should I get Cal?"

Efren sat and put the foldable keyboard on his lap, dulling the sound even more. She thought he was being paranoid. There was no way Cal didn't make this place soundproof, but she supposed, considering his job, safer was better than sorry. She waited while he typed out what he'd seen and then asked her if she had an update.

What was written had her seeing red. "His lawyers filed a writ of habeas corpus?"

Efren turned to her. "What is that? I'm not a law enforcement person."

"Unlawful imprisonment," she answered. "Ask her if she knows the content of the writ."

After typing, they waited for Mina to answer. It wasn't one Selina liked, and Efren must have sensed it. "She may not know yet, but give her time, and she will find out what it is."

"It won't do us any good if we aren't in contact with her by the time she knows." The words were hissed through her teeth. She wasn't mad at him, it wasn't his fault, but she was mad that Randall's lawyers were playing games. The man deserved to rot in prison for his crimes—both the ones they knew about and the ones they didn't. Letting him out of prison was a surefire way of having him disappear, leaving her on the run forever.

Selina grabbed the keyboard from him and typed her own question. "When does he go before the judge?"

"Monday."

Selina did the math in her head and realized they were coming up on early Thursday morning. "That doesn't give us much time," she whispered, her lips in a thin line as she typed back to Mina. "As soon as you know, I have to know." Mina gave her a thumbs-up and then stood, moving aside so Cal could sit down.

Selina paced the room. She wanted to pay attention, but her mind was still focused on Randall. If his lawyers had proof that he was being unlawfully detained, he could go free as soon as Monday. Since she hadn't been present for the trial, she had no idea if that was a possibility. Then again, she knew the Snake, and chances were good that money was changing hands as they spoke.

"Colvert," Efren whispered, and she snapped to attention. He was motioning her over and she leaned in next to him. "You and Cal need to talk strategy."

"Strategy? Isn't that your call?"

"This is your life, you should have a say in it, yes?"

She took his seat and pulled the keyboard onto her lap. Cal was speaking, and she waited for the captions to come up.

Avoid going west. Once you leave the state, it will be harder for me to help. You're much closer to the western border, so go east or southeast.

Do you have another safe house in any direction of this location?

Negative. You have experience with avoiding Vaccaro

in the past. Fall back on that. Once you're clear, call in and we'll have a plan in place.

Selina frowned as she stared at the man who had given her a home, sharpened her skills and treated her like family the last eight years. *Is leaving the bunker the right decision, or should we stay put?*

What does your gut say? Cal asked.

Run. Three letters. One word. The story of her life.

Now you're in your element. Good luck, Sierra. Charlie, out.

Before she could wrap her head around the fact that might be the last time she ever spoke to her friend, a low, guttural curse came from Efren's side of the console. He pointed at the top left camera where one of the four guys was spinning the hatch open inside the old cabin. He held his finger to his lips, and she nodded, watching in silence as one of the men climbed down the ladder and inspected the small space. There was barely room for him to turn around, which meant he wouldn't see the camera hidden inside one of the pipes. They didn't miss the shot of his face, though. They captured it and Efren sent it to Mina for identification. The night-vision goggles might make that more difficult, but if Mina could get his name, she would.

The guy climbed the ladder and shook his head at his buddies. After whispered conversation they weren't privy to, the men broke off into teams of two again and spread out through the woods, headed back in the direction of the Jeep. Once they disappeared, Efren let out a breath.

"Chances are they're going to regroup at the Jeep and fan out in the next direction," he whispered.

"Which will make it hard to know which way to go, right?"

He waited another few minutes until the teams were past the second set of cameras in the woods, then he waited a few more minutes after that, she assumed to make sure they didn't come back again. Once an adequate amount of time had passed, he started unplugging and unhooking several devices.

"These are going with us. They're our only tie to Secure One."

Selina held her bag out for him to stow away the folding keyboard and receiver. Once safely tucked away in protective pockets, she closed the bag and lowered it to the ground. "What's the plan, Brenna?"

"You tell me. I'm following your lead."

Her nod was almost imperceptible, but it gave her the push she needed to make the decision. "I don't know how you feel about it, but I don't want to be here if they come back during the day and find our hatch."

"Same. Walk me through the plan."

"We know they're out there, but this is our only window. We'll give them a thirty-minute head start. It took us an hour to get here from the Jeep, but I was moving much slower than they were tonight. We know they're headed north. We can't be sure where they'll go from there, but my bet is north or west, thinking we'll head for the closest border. If we head southeast, we'll be clear of them before daybreak. What say you, Brenna?"

"I say, I'll follow you anywhere, Colvert."

Before she could react, he dragged her toward him by the back of her head until their lips collided in a kiss that heated to boiling instantly. If they were going to survive this, she would have to keep her lips off his. When he tipped his head to take the kiss deeper, she knew that was going to be easier said than done.

THE SUN WAS breaking on the horizon, and they'd been walking for nearly five hours. Efren could see Selina needed to rest sooner rather than later. She'd been a trouper keeping pace with him all night, but as 6:00 a.m. approached, she needed food, a place to sit down, and a few more Advil before they could continue their journey.

He followed her down along a shallow creek and started edging her closer to the road. They needed to find a restaurant where they could sit for a bit and give her side time to rest. First, they had to get close enough to the road to watch for civilization. He hoped she was tired enough that she wouldn't notice what he was doing. It was easy to let her lead. She was an excellent leader who thought of even the smallest things that could trip them up, but she wasn't good at admitting when she needed rest. She would push herself until she crossed the line, and then he'd be finding a hospital instead of a diner.

Their walk had been in silence, and he'd spent the majority of it replaying that last kiss they'd shared in the bunker before risking their lives to save them. He hadn't held back that time and moved it past closed-lipped and into territory he wasn't sure she wanted to go, until she'd willingly joined him in the hot tangle of tongues. When the kiss ended and they made their plans for leaving the bunker, he'd vowed to keep his hands and his lips to himself going forward, but nothing turned him on more than a strong, independent woman who could take care of herself. Selina Colvert was that and so much more.

Maybe that was how he should look at his time with Selina. Whatever happened between them happened because the feelings were mutual, but that didn't mean there were strings attached when the case ended. His hard and fast rule had always been never to get involved with anyone he was guarding, but Selina wasn't just anyone. She was a teammate, an equal, dare he say a friend now that they'd put their trust, and lives, in each other's hands.

"Brenna," Selina hissed from his left. "You're too close to the road. Fall back."

Well, he should have known she wouldn't miss his migration east. "We need to find someplace to rest. I'm watching for signs to a diner or a gas station."

"Negative," she whispered, grabbing his backpack to pull him to a stop. "What part of 'we can't be seen' do you not understand? We may have left those guys behind, but they aren't the only guys. Vaccaro has scouts all over this state, I can assure you."

"That may well be true, but you aren't going to make it much farther without resting. We need food and to check your incision."

"Fine," she said, pointing ahead. "We'll cross the creek up there and stop as soon as the sun is up. That will allow us to rebandage the wounds without using a flashlight and we can grab a protein bar and some water."

"Or," he said, taking her hand and keeping her level with him as he continued to walk closer to the road. "We can find someplace big enough that we can blend in and grab something hot to eat. It would be good to have hot water and soap so we don't get your wound infected."

She held up until he had to stop or risk pulling her over. "What happened to 'you're in charge, Colvert. You know this guy best'?"

Efren spun on his heel and tipped her chin up. "I stand by that until I see you pushing yourself too far. Then you start making bad decisions that can make your situation worse. I've watched you go from a five to a six to a seven on the pain scale in the last two hours. It's time to rest your body."

"Now you're an expert on my pain scale?"

The sarcasm dripped from the sentence when she crossed her arms over her chest and waited for him to respond.

"Yes, because I saw you at ten when I forced you to walk through the woods for an hour after a perilous ride less than a day after surgery. I've cataloged in my mind what level of pain you're at when you take medication and when you don't. I may not be an expert on you, but I'm observant, and that's what keeps people alive when I protect them. While I stand behind you running the show with how Vaccaro will behave, and knowing the best way to avoid him, keeping you safe is still my job. I will override you with a snap of my fingers if I think you're putting yourself at risk." He snapped his fingers in front of her face and she jumped, but not before he noticed the smoke in her eyes catch a flame.

Good. Let her get fired up. That would keep her going until they got somewhere to rest.

Selina stepped up to him and put her finger on his chest. "If you think I can't deal with a little bit of pain, you're dead wrong. I'm going to hurt much worse if Vaccaro gets hold of me—"

A stick snapped to the left of them, announcing in no uncertain terms that they weren't alone.

Chapter Eleven

Selina slowly removed her finger from Efren's chest and reached for her gun as he did the same. The woods had fallen silent again and they waited, their only communication their eyes. "Could be an animal," he mouthed, and she nodded. It could be an animal. It could be a snake.

She motioned with her eyes to a tree less than five feet behind them. They just had to make it there without alerting anyone that they were so close. The detritus on the forest floor was going to make that difficult, but they needed cover in case whatever was in the woods was an animal that walked on two legs and carried a big gun.

His nod was slow and deliberate as he brought his hand up to point from his eyes to the woods, telling her he'd watch while she went first. There was no way to argue with him, and he was supposed to be her bodyguard, so she looked down at her feet and slowly inched her way toward the tree. It was a giant oak that would easily hide them from anyone walking past, as long as they didn't get too close. It felt like forever before she had her back plastered to the tree. She inhaled a breath, then slowly turned and stuck her gun around the side of the tree, a sign to Efren to move.

He had taken his first step when the first shot rang out. Efren used it for cover and tore at her, rolling behind the tree as the second shot hit the dirt not too far from where they were standing.

"Not an animal," he hissed as they each braced their gun around opposite sides of the tree.

"What's the plan, bodyguard?"

"As much as I hate to say it, we wait." He eyed his bag. "You're going to need a bigger gun."

He'd been carrying an assault rifle through the woods, while she'd kept her sidearm on her only. Carrying an extra eight pounds around her shoulder would wear her out too quickly, so he'd kept it on his pack. Selina slowly holstered her sidearm and reached for the gun as another shot peppered the ground to the left of the tree.

Haste had her grabbing the gun off his pack and bringing it up to her shoulder in one smooth motion. "Where are they shooting from?"

"I can't tell. The vegetation is too thick this time of year. Until they show their face, we can't shoot back in case it's an innocent."

"They're shooting at us!"

"They could think we're an animal."

Selina couldn't stop the eye roll. "It's not even hunting season. We need to move."

"Not until we know where they are," he hissed, his words barely audible in the silence of the forest. "We could be surrounded."

She hated that he was right, but he was. Just because the bullets were coming from in front of them didn't mean there wasn't a team on every side. They didn't have enough ammo for a gunfight of that size, so she had to hope that wasn't the case. There were four last night, and she had to pray there were only four this morning. She glanced at Efren, who had his gun up without a waver as he waited, sweeping the dark vegetation in front of them.

"Slowly bend down and find something to throw to your right," he whispered.

Drawing fire was an excellent way to determine their location. She searched around the tree for something to throw until she encountered a hefty rock. With a nod to him, she tossed it to the right, and it landed and rolled a few feet before someone lit it up. She wasn't expecting the pop-pop from next to her but was happy he had a shot. Then she heard a grunt, and a heavy object dropped to the forest floor.

Her eyes wide, she glanced at Efren, who used the suppressor on his rifle to point at the ground, and then he mouthed, "throw another."

The man was going to pick them off one after the other to protect her. She felt around and came up with a piece of bark. It wasn't big, but at least it wouldn't sound the same as the rock. Efren gave her a head nod and she tossed it to their left. The morning was immediately lit up by gunfire, and he used the illumination to send a few bullets their way until they heard another body hit the ground.

"They aren't the smartest blokes in the forest," he muttered.

"That's Vaccaro men for ya," she whispered with a grin. The situation wasn't funny, but leave it to Efren to ease her fear a little bit.

"Throw something else. I doubt they'll take the bait again, but we have to try."

She grabbed a rock and tossed it far to the right. They waited, but this time, nothing happened. They stood in silence another five minutes, but they couldn't wait all day. They had to make a decision.

"We need to move, Brenna," she said, gun in hand. "Last night, there were two teams of two. Maybe they split up."

"That's what I'm thinking, too. Back-to-back until we know for sure."

"What direction?" she asked, lining their backpacks up and sweeping her gun across the trees in front of her.

"To find the hunters who became the hunted."

Efren moved forward, and Selina followed, struggling to walk backward without falling on the uneven terrain. Her trained ear listened for footfalls or any sound to indicate another human in the woods. They were barely across the creek and into the deeper vegetation again when moaning reached their ears. He tipped his head twice to the right, and they sidestepped toward the sound, watching for an ambush. It wasn't likely, or the bullets would have rained down on them already.

She nearly tripped and fell on the first body until Efren tossed his arm back to grab her. Once she was solid again, he stuck his left leg out while he crouched on his right to check the guy's pulse.

"Dead." He put his finger to his lips and tipped his ear to the side to indicate they should listen.

Selina heard a soft gurgling and motioned forward and to the right frantically. The guy was still alive, but he wouldn't be for long. Efren held her back and followed the sound at the same pace, sweeping his gun across the brightening forest as the sun rose above them. The light revealed the man they were looking for as he lay against a tree trunk, blood running from his neck and mouth with every labored breath.

Efren motioned to the left, and she turned and brought her gun up as he knelt by the man. "Who are you and what do you want with us?"

"Her," he said, his hand slowly raising to point at Selina. "He wants her."

"Who's he?" Efren asked, but Selina didn't wait with bated breath. She already knew the answer.

The man hissed, then laughed, blood bubbling out of his mouth with the action. "He's coming for you, little Eva Shannon. You once were lost, but now you're found."

"How many more are there?" Efren asked the question but the man just smiled, as though his secret was her death sentence. Efren pressed the butt of his gun to the guy's neck wound. "I'm going to ask you one more time. How many are there?"

"None today," he croaked as Efren eased off on the gun. "Tomorrow, more than you can count and the next day, even more. You can't escape the Snake, sweet Eva. Tag, you're it. Run, run, as fast as you ca…"

The sentence hung in the air as the guy's head lolled to the side and a final breath left his body. Efren cursed and grabbed his flashlight, shining it across the body frantically.

"GPS," she whispered and ran to the other guy, searching his body for the tracker he likely wore. If they had activated it before they went down, Vaccaro would send reinforcements. It took a moment but then she spotted it. "Left side of the vest!"

Selina pulled his off and ran back to Efren, who was

struggling. She helped him and then motioned for him to follow her. He did without question, this time taking the back position while she walked forward at a fast clip. She held up her fist in a stop motion and slung her gun around her chest. A fast dig through his pack, and she came up with a condom. They used them at Secure One for all types of things from water containers to boot liners. She had something else in mind as she rolled the condom over the beacons, blew air into it, and tied it off. Once she was satisfied with the vessel, she lowered it to the creek and let it go.

"Brilliant," Efren said with a chuckle as the beacons floated downstream at a leisurely walking pace.

"All that does is buy us time." Selina stood and shook her head as the sun came up. "The guy was right. This place will be crawling with snakes faster than we can kill them. We have to find a faster way to move."

"Agreed. For now, let's move as quick as we can the opposite direction of those beacons."

He took off at a pace that was going to be tough for her to match, but she dug deep and reminded herself if she didn't find a way, she would find herself in the snake's den, and the pain would be greater than anything she had dealt with thus far.

HER BODY WAS screaming at her, but she wouldn't stop. Couldn't stop until they had a place to hole up long enough to take a shower and contact Secure One. A little food wouldn't hurt, either. Efren was trailing her, not demanding answers, which surprised her if she were honest. He had been incredibly supportive of her plans, only pushing back when he wanted her to stop long enough to think about things from all angles. They hadn't had time for her to do that when they hopped a ride in an old potato truck about four hours ago. They didn't know where he was going, but it was better than where they were at the time. It afforded them time off their feet to rest their bodies while getting as far away from the two dead guys as quickly as possible. When the truck stopped to refuel, they opted to jump out and find a place to contact Secure One. Mina was their eyes in the sky, and they needed more information. Hopefully, she had it.

"Where are we going?" Efren asked, his voice nearly drowned out by the rushing of the Mississippi River. The Mighty Miss was raging today, and that told Selina a storm was coming. Actually, more than one storm was coming for them, which was why they needed to regroup and get better prepared.

"I'll know it when I see it." That was the only answer she could give since she hadn't found what she was looking for yet.

They'd taken a few more steps when her arm shot out in front of them. "There."

"A cabin?" He pulled her to a stop and forced her to make eye contact. "Why?"

"It's November, so the cabins are closed for the winter. At least that one is. With any luck, inside is a shower, food and a place to call home."

"Fine, but let me scout it. Better I'm caught on camera than you."

Selina wanted to argue, but she couldn't. He was right. She had to be a ghost if she wanted to survive long enough to clear this area and get back to Secure One alive. He tugged his gaiter up around his face to hide it the best he could before he leaned in to whisper, "If it's safe, I'll owl call."

With a nod from her, he took off, approaching the cabin from behind where cameras would be less likely. Selina watched the way he moved across the yard. Considering he'd been on his leg for almost a full day and still moved like a dancer, it was impressive. He disappeared around the end of the cabin, and she waited for him to pop back up at the front of the place. When he did, he was low and angled away from any cameras that might be pointing right at him. He moved in slowly, knowing that any doorbell with a camera would be easy to spot on a cabin this old.

She moved closer, her trained eye already knowing the cabin was as low-tech as they come. Her validation came in the form of an owl hoot from the porch of the small structure. By the time she joined him, he was holding up a key.

"Guess they aren't afraid of theft." He had the door open and held up his finger, doing a quick sweep of the three-room cabin before he motioned her in. "Shades."

In quick succession they pulled the shades and then dropped their packs. "I'm glad we found this place. A storm is blowing in." Selina unzipped her coat and pulled her gaiter off as she took a look around. "Doesn't look like anyone has been here for quite a few seasons."

"That was the vibe I got, too, by looking in the windows. Let's just hope no one decides now is the time to take a trip to Grandpa's cabin."

"Not likely this late in the season with a storm brewing. We need to get a call into Secure One now before we can't." To make her point, a gust of wind rattled the windowpanes and made her jump.

"Hey, it's okay." Efren walked over and rubbed her arms before he pulled her into a quick hug. "You did good, Colvert. I'm proud of you for not only hanging on but finding the opportunities we needed to get clear of that mess. Let's use this time to regroup and make our next plan."

"I'm glad we got the best of those two in the woods, but there will be more."

"I know." He kissed her cheek before he stepped back and held her out at arm's length. "We're a team, and we'll face whatever comes at us the same way we did with those guys. Together."

"I'd be screwed without you, Brenna."

"Did it hurt to admit that?" he asked, his lips quirking in humor.

"Surprisingly, no. I've taken many of my frustrations out on you for too long. You didn't deserve it, but you were convenient. When you went to bat for me with Cal in the bunker, I realized you didn't deserve attitude from me."

"Apology accepted." He winked while he set out the equipment to call Secure One. "I'm a big boy and always knew there was more to your dislike of me than met the eye."

He fell silent as though he were waiting for her to tell him what that was, but she had no intention of doing that, now or ever. Admitting that she didn't hate him was hard, but admitting that she cared about him in ways she shouldn't could be dangerous to her heart and her life.

Chapter Twelve

She had bigger fish to fry than Efren Brenna's ego, and his name was Vaccaro. Selina made a vow to remind herself of that every minute of every hour if need be. The console linked up, and Efren spoke.

"Secure one, Tango."

"Secure two, Whiskey," came the voice of an angel.

Selina dropped to the small couch in relief. "Secure three, Sierra."

The small screen came to life, and Mina's face reflected at them, grainy and barely visible, but smiling. She panned the camera out, and four other faces stared back at them. Cal, Mack, Roman and Eric also sat around the table. "So good to see you guys!" Mina said. "We've been cautiously optimistic you'd call soon."

"Is that your way of saying you've been worried?" Efren's question was in good fun, but Mina nodded immediately.

"More than worried, especially when you missed your check-in," Cal said.

"Sorry about that. We were in the back of a potato truck moving too fast for the phone."

"A potato truck? Never mind, I don't want to know. Fill us in."

Efren was about to speak when Selina did. "We ran into two of Vaccaro's guys about four hours south of the bunker. Mr. Sharpshooter over here took them both out with a shot."

"Before they died, one confirmed they were working for the Snake and that more were on their way."

"That's when we jumped on the potato truck," Selina said to clarify. "We had to get out of the area quickly and without being seen."

"I'm relieved you found a way out," Roman said. "What's your location?"

"The Mississippi is right outside the window. That's all I know, other than the name of the gas station the truck stopped at. We borrowed a cabin until the storm passes."

"Borrowed," Mina said with a snort. "I'm glad you found shelter. We have much to discuss and little time to do it. First, tell me the name of the gas station."

"Go for It Gas," Selina said as Efren laughed. "What?" She punched his arm playfully. "It was easy to remember."

Mina clicked the keyboard a few times and then smiled. "You're on the outskirts of Winona to the north. That's a good place to be. Now, let's fill you in on Daddy Dearest."

Selina leaned in toward the console. "Do we know why he's being released?"

"We do, or at least why he's going before the judge. I'm glad you're sitting down. The writ of habeas corpus they filed pertains to you."

"Me?" she asked, and Mina nodded with a grimace.

"Randall's original trial lawyer allowed your written

testimony to be included in the trial paperwork despite
it not being signed. He also didn't ask the prosecuting
team to do the due diligence of finding your body."

"Is that a thing?" Efren asked, glancing at her.

Mina nodded. "It is, but I don't buy it. I suspect
money has changed hands here and this is just a way to
get Daddy Dearest out of prison."

"Why now, though?" Efren asked in confusion. "It's
been years."

"Because Randall Jr. was arrested." Selina's answer
was resigned. "Vaccaro probably planned this all along,
and we walked right into the trap he set."

"I don't understand," everyone said at once.

"Explain it if you can," Efren encouraged her, and she
stood, pacing back and forth behind him as the winds
intensified.

"The Snake was setting Randall Jr. up to take a fall by
killing Howie. There's no way to know for sure, but if Junior wasn't running the counterfeiting business the way
Vaccaro wanted, or heaven forbid, was skimming off the
top, he would make an example out of him. Since Howie
was already cheating on the Winged Templar's daughter, it was easy to kill him. They drop his body in the
storage unit since Sadie works there and set up Sadie to
take the fall, already knowing that Randall had Kadie."

"He had no way to know we would be there that night,
though," Eric said.

"As I said, we fell into his trap. We played his game
perfectly. In the end, Randall was arrested on kidnap-
ping charges, which will put him away for life. With
Randall Jr. and Howie both out of the picture, Vaccaro
needs someone to run the business. Now it's time to

get Daddy out after having served just enough years to make it look like an injustice was corrected rather than a criminal walked. The original trial attorney left that unsigned statement of mine in there on purpose. It was planted for this very occasion. I'm honestly surprised Vaccaro didn't just kill Randall Jr. and be done with it."

Cal's gaze darted to Mina's, and Selina cleared her throat. "What?"

"They found Junior unresponsive in his jail cell this morning. He's not dead, but he's also not expected to live."

Selina threw her arms up. "More reason for Daddy to get out of prison. Now he's lost two sons since he was so unjustly incarcerated. I should have signed that statement before I started writing it!"

"Was there a reason you hadn't signed it?" Efren asked, taking her hand and leading her to the couch to sit. "Rest. You're still healing."

"I didn't sign it because I wasn't finished with it. I had it on my desk and was working on it when I got called in and suspended for the shooting. Once that happens, I'm not allowed back into the area for anything. They must have found it on my desk, but I don't know anyone who would have put a half-finished, unsigned statement in a trial packet, cop or lawyer alike."

"Remember when we talked about someone being a mole for Vaccaro?" Efren said, and she nodded. "This smells like a mole."

"It smells like a rat." Cal's voice was angry. "And snakes love nothing more than a rat for a snack."

"I'll look into it," Mina said, writing it down on her pad.

"Did you find anything about Randall Jr.'s arrest before his unfortunate accident?" Efren asked.

"He used his one phone call for his lawyer. That was it."

"Vaccaro likely pays his lawyer, so any mention of the missing twin being in his basement that night would easily flow back to the snake's den," Cal said. "For now, that's our working theory. We assume he knows Selina is alive from the lawyer and sent Ava to clean that mess up. Since she couldn't, he's hunting you while trying to free his head capo."

"Just another day in the life," Selina said with an eye roll.

"We have the information. What's our next move?" Efren asked, sitting beside Selina and putting his arm around her waist. She glanced at him questioningly, but he didn't seem bothered by his PDA in front of the team. Thankfully, only Mina seemed to have noticed the interaction when she looked back to the console.

"There's more," Mina said, holding up her finger and pointing at Roman, who held up a map of Minnesota. "It turns out, the house in Bemidji isn't the only property titled in Randall Sr.'s name."

"What?" Selina asked, leaning in to see the grainy video.

"I did some digging and discovered a house in Caledonia that Randall owns." Roman held the map up to the screen so they could see the house marked near Highway 44.

"Wait," Efren said, his eyes roving in his head for a minute. "If we're near Winona, that puts Caledonia somewhere around fifty klicks from here."

"It's close, for sure," Cal said, leaning forward, ready to take over. "We can't be certain, since we can't do much recon on the place, but our guess is that's where Randall Jr. moved the operation after the trial. He couldn't keep anything in the Bemidji place, but as long as he lived there, he could make authorities believe he was clean."

"Did Randall Jr. travel to Caledonia frequently?" Eric asked, suddenly interested in the conversation again.

"Not as often as Howie Loraine did prior to his untimely beheading."

"Interesting," Selina said. "Maybe Howie was the gopher to keep Junior's nose clean."

"Possible," Cal agreed. "What are you thinking? I can see your instincts are locked and loaded on this. You know the family and how the Snake runs. We're counting on you to tell us our next move."

Selina was silent for a moment. She hoped they thought she was thinking of a plan instead of trying not to cry. She'd longed to hear Cal say those words. To treat her as an equal. To acknowledge her skills as a cop and law enforcement professional. Now that he was, she was afraid to screw it up. All she ever wanted was for them to see her as an equal. Suddenly, she was at a loss for words.

"Follow your gut," Efren whispered in her ear. "It's telling you the right answer."

His words broke her internal freeze-up, and she nodded. "If he's released by the judge on Monday, and you think he will be?" She was addressing Mina, who nodded. "They'll do one of two things. Go to one of Vaccaro's places and regroup, or go to Caledonia."

"Which do you think is more likely?"

"Hard to know if I can't see the place in Caledonia."

Mina held up her finger and dug around in a pile by her computer, coming up with a paper she handed to Roman. He held it up to the camera. "I could only get a view from above, but as you can see it's—"

"Sprawling," Efren said.

"There," Selina said without conscious thought. "They'll go there. Ava's a spoiled brat. When she showed up at the hospital in a fur coat, it was obvious to me she hadn't changed her spots. She wants the cushy lifestyle, and that place affords them her every whim. Of that, I'm certain."

"Now that's your gut talking," Efren whispered, squeezing her hip.

"I'm inclined to agree with you," Cal said. "Not regarding Ava, but that Randall will want to check his operation immediately."

"Vaccaro will demand it," Selina said, standing to pace again. "It's been unattended or left in the care of an underling for too long. What time on Monday?"

"The docket says 11:00 a.m."

She paced a few more times, and an idea came to her that was dangerous but diabolical. "What if I was also there at 11:00 a.m. to give my sworn statement to the court? Signed, sealed and delivered."

"Not going to happen!" Efren said, jumping up and grasping her arms as though he forgot they weren't alone in the room. "Are you trying to get yourself killed?"

"The court would protect me. Is it dangerous, yes, but it would keep Randall Sr. in prison."

"Which doesn't solve our problem." It was Cal's voice, this time from behind them. She couldn't break eye contact with Efren. What she saw in his eyes said maybe he cared about her as more than just a job. "Randall is still in jail, but Ava and the Snake won't be. Doing that signs your death warrant, too."

"He's right," Efren said between clenched teeth. "You know he's right. We've fought too hard to keep you alive. We think this out. We make the plan and then we follow it. If we don't, you won't make it out of that courtroom alive. We both know it. You always want to do the right thing, and I'm proud as hell of you for even suggesting it, even knowing you'd be giving up your life for it, but you'd be giving up your life for the low-hanging fruit. We need the apple at the top of the tree, and the only way to get that is to let the rotten apple out of prison."

"As long as Ava is free, she will hunt me, Efren. We can't live that kind of life. I've been hiding for years from Vaccaro. I can't hide forever."

"If that's the case," Cal said from behind them, "Brenna is right. Let Randall out of prison; get him back to Caledonia. If they're both there, then we have evidence that Ava knows about the operation."

"What did you just say?" Selina asked, spinning on her heel.

"That we'd have proof Ava knows about the operation."

Selina smacked herself in the forehead. "Of course she does! That's where she's been all this time."

"You think Vaccaro was letting her run the operation all these years?"

"Hell no." Her laughter was enough to make Efren smile, she noticed. "There's no way he'd trust a Shannon to run any of his operations. Even one who had proven herself to his organization. That doesn't mean she wasn't living there all this time and helping. It's the only thing that makes sense."

"You think there's proof there that she knew the operation had continued all these years?" Roman asked, and Selina nodded. "If that's the case, and we can find it, it would take one assassin off your heels."

"Just not the most dangerous one," Selina said, gnawing on her lip. "There's no 'we' here, either." She dropped her hands and leaned into the console. "I won't put any of you at risk again. This is not your war to fight, and God knows you've all lost enough fighting other people's wars. This is my problem and my problem alone. From the moment I saw Ava standing at the nurses' station, I knew my days were numbered. There is no escaping the reach the Snake has when your time comes. My time has come to face off with this cobra, and I accept that. I can't accept anyone else getting hurt because of me."

"He's a man," Cal said, standing to his full height and leaning into the camera. "Not a god. He is not untouchable, Selina Colvert, and this team is damn good at its job. We protect and we serve, we just do it a bit differently than you're used to. That doesn't mean we don't get results. The storm is ramping up and we're about to lose connection. Stay put. Rest. Prepare. As soon as the storm is over, call in. We'll have an actionable plan. Do you understand me, Sierra?"

Selina wanted to argue, but knew it would do no good. "Understood."

"Good. Charlie, out."

The screen went blank, and she looked up into the

eyes of the man who had gotten her this far, but could end up a casualty of her past. She wasn't okay with that.

"I'm okay with it," he said, as though he were reading her mind. "I've fought less just wars than the one we're about to wade into, Colvert."

"Vaccaro has an army of soldiers, Efren." She was desperate to make him understand. "This is another war you can't win, but this time you'll pay with your life. If you send me alone, then no innocents have to die."

His finger came down on her lips to hush her. "He may have an army of soldiers, but they protect him for money. We protect you for love. That's why he will fail and you won't. Never forget that."

Chapter Thirteen

He shouldn't have used the L-word. He saw it in her eyes the moment he'd said it. She was dealing with enough, and that put pressure on her that she didn't need. Not that he meant it in a romantic sense, not using "we" before it, but she was an intelligent woman who was good at reading between the lines after working with men all her life. There was nothing he could do about it now other than continue to reassure her that the team was behind her and not going to let her face Vaccaro alone.

When Selina disappeared into the small bathroom to clean up, Efren had rummaged around the kitchen in hopes of finding some kind of canned good that was still edible. He wasn't expecting to pull open the fridge and encounter someone's canning stash. Why it was in the fridge, he had no idea, but he wasn't going to look a gift horse in the mouth. Admittedly, he held his breath when he tried to light the stove, fearing the propane tank in the backyard had long been empty. He was pleasantly surprised when it lit up and he was able to warm their dinner. The temperature was dropping outside, so rather than freeze the entire night, he'd also started the small propane cabin heater on low. He didn't know how long the propane would last, but it was better to warm up the cabin for as long as possible. If the propane ran out, they'd stay warm the rest of the night with the blankets from the bedroom. Always a gentleman, he'd give her the bed to sleep while he kept watch. He wasn't worried, though. The storm raging outside wasn't fit for man nor beast, but most especially not Vaccaro's men. The wind whipped against the cabin walls, and the river roared her way past them. Anyone out there tonight had a death wish.

"What smells so good?" Selina asked as she walked into the room. She was wearing a sweatshirt and pants that were too big for her, but she had the shirt tied in a knot to show her midriff and the pants cuffed at the ankles.

The sight of her bare midriff had him staring rather than speaking. "Uh, dinner," he was finally able to stutter. "What's with the outfit?"

"I found clothes in the dresser in there that were warm and clean. Saved a pair for you, too. I was surprised that there was warm water."

"Propane tank," he said, his throat still dry as he stared at the incision on her belly. "I thought it would be empty, but it's not. Shouldn't you have a bandage on that?"

Efren motioned her to the table where he had two sets of silverware waiting. She sat and he carried the hot pot of stew over, with veggies and brown bread for their feast.

"Dang," Selina whispered low when he set out the food. "Did you make a run to Winn-Dixie?"

He snorted as he slid into his seat. "I'd have to go pretty far to find a Winn-Dixie around here. I found all of this in the fridge. They were storing it in there. I thought that was a bit odd."

"Mmm," she said, taking a bite of the bread and chewing. "Not odd. An unplugged fridge will keep the canned goods from freezing in the winter if there's no heat. Then you just move them back to the shelf in the spring."

"I thought if there was no heat then there was no water? Why is there running water?"

"Insulated pipes," she answered around a bite of beef stew. "These cabins are mainly for summer, but a lot of trappers and snow lovers use them throughout the seasons. I feel like whoever owns this place isn't one of them. They come early spring through late fall."

"We can hope." He glanced at the door again, and she laughed.

"No one is coming out tonight. Was the barricade necessary?"

He glanced at the door again, where he'd shoved a heavy chest full of raincoats and other fishing equipment against it. "Yes. It won't stop anyone, but it will slow them down enough for us to bail out the bedroom window. We still need to avoid light hitting any of the windows. I'm sure the neighbors are also long gone, but we can't risk it."

"Penlights only, aimed at the floor. Oh, this is so good," she moaned as she took another bite of the bread. "I haven't had canned brown bread in years."

"I'll admit when I saw that I thought it was one of those fake cans where you hide your valuables or something. Never saw anything like it when that bread came out onto the plate."

"Are you from Mars?"

"California," he answered, and her lips tipped up on one side.

"That explains it."

"California explains why I've never seen bread in a can?"

"It's a Boston thing that's moved west, but probably not quite that far west. We keep it handy for power outages and snowstorms. The carbs keep you going, and you can eat it straight out of the can."

"I've eaten much worse meals ready to eat." He pointed at her belly. "Why isn't that bandaged?"

"I'm letting it get some air," she explained between bites. "The skin is red around the stitches, so after dinner, we're going to have to remove them."

"Remove them?" He propped his spoon in his bowl. "It's only been seven days since the surgery."

"Plenty long for my skin. I heal fast. If I let them go too long, they'll fester until they're infected. Trust me. I've had enough stitches in my life to know."

"I'm going to need more than a penlight to get them out."

"The bathroom doesn't have a window," she said. "We can close the door and get it done. I can do the front ones. You'll have to do the back ones."

He shuddered, drawing a laugh from her as she finished her stew. "The big bad bodyguard can't handle a few stitches?"

"Reminds me of my military days. Getting stitches in the field, or watching them desperately try to stitch a friend's body part closed long enough to get them to safety before they bled out." He cleared his throat and stood. "I found some cinnamon applesauce for dessert. Let me grab it."

As he walked away from her, he shoved the memories bubbling up inside him back behind the black curtain. Every so often, they liked to peek their head around the corner to remind him why he didn't *care*. Caring led to pain. He'd had more than enough of that for a lifetime.

EFREN PACED THE front porch, holding the sat phone in his hand. He'd left Selina inside to stay warm with the excuse that he needed to check the phone for messages. The storm had slowed for a bit, but there was still no way to get coverage inside the cabin. Would there be any messages? No, but he wasn't looking for them. He wanted to call Secure One when she wasn't within earshot so he could suggest a plan he knew she would never agree to.

The cold sleet pellets pounded on his back as he dialed Cal's secure phone. The phone didn't even ring before he heard, "Secure one, Charlie."

"Secure two, Tango," he answered. It sounded like a greeting, but it wasn't. It was a go-ahead between team members that it was safe to speak. If they answered any other way, they knew the team member was being tracked or held by the enemy. Considering what Cal used to do before he started Secure One, it was a legitimate way to ensure everyone's safety.

"Everything okay?" Cal asked. "I'm surprised to hear from you again, but I'm glad you called. I need your opinion on how Selina is doing after the surgery."

"Storm is raging here, as I'm sure you can hear. We just finished removing her stitches."

"Already? It's been seven days."

"Exactly what I said, but she's completely healed. Most bizarre thing I've ever seen. Do you know how many times she's been shot?"

"I suspected this wasn't the first," Cal said with a chuckle. "She was way too calm when she climbed out of that hole."

"To answer your question, she's in decent shape considering a bullet to the gut. She has a good appetite and has semi-okay stamina. The less walking we have to do, the better, though, for me and her."

"Noted. I know you don't have your other leg. How are you holding up?"

Efren bit his tongue to keep from telling the truth about his limb. They had bigger problems to solve, and his whining wasn't going to help. "Good. I can wear both legs interchangeably, though the blade can tire me out faster if I wear it too long. I'll be fine until this is resolved. Before we lose our connection, I need to talk to you about something when Selina isn't around."

"Of course you have my permission to date her. Not that you need it."

"I'm sorry?" He couldn't hold in his laughter.

"You aren't calling to ask me for her hand in marriage?"

"Smart-ass," Efren grumped as the cold wind whipped hard against his neck. "No, I'm calling to suggest we keep the cops out of the situation in Caledonia."

"What's your reason?"

"If the chance is given, we need to take out Vaccaro and Ava. Cops make that messy."

"Not untrue, but also, we aren't cops, and that's breaking the law."

"Oh, come on," Efren huffed, burrowing deeper into his coat to block the rain. "How many times in your life have you had to do bad things to benefit the greater good?"

"Too many, but does killing the Snake and Ava benefit the greater good or does it benefit Selina?"

Efren bit his lip and stepped closer to the cabin to keep from getting drenched. He was glad he'd saved his shower until after he made the call. He was going to need it. "It can't benefit both?"

"That depends on who comes out better off. Selina or the greater good."

Efren took a deep breath to keep from losing his temper with his boss. "It's like you want this guy to kill Selina, and he will, if we don't get to him first."

"Listen here, Brenna. The very last thing I want is to lose Selina from the team. She's paramount to everything we do here and while she may not see that, the rest of us do. I would take Vaccaro out with my bare hands if given the chance, but I can't risk the reputation of Secure One and what I've built here. What's the saying, cut off the head of a snake and a new one will take its place?"

Efren wasn't giving up. If they brought the cops in on this mission, Selina was going to die. "If the head of the snake is removed, you can bet the rest of the heads will be too busy scrambling to wonder where Selina Colvert has gone. All I'm asking is to wait and loop the cops in on this operation after the fact rather than before."

"Does Selina know you're asking this of the team?"

"Not yet."

Cal was silent, and Efren had to wonder what he was thinking. It was a big ask, but Selina would never be safe if they didn't stop Ava and Vaccaro. She deserved more out of life than constantly looking over her shoulder for the next bullet.

"I'll keep the cops out of our plans for now," Cal finally said. "For now. That could change depending on what we find when we get to Caledonia. Understood?"

"Loud and clear," Efren said, letting out a breath.

"Selina has always been the one to demand we bring the cops in. I'm not sure how she's going to feel about you going behind her back like this."

"Let me handle Selina. Do you have an actionable plan?"

"Working on it," Cal answered. "As soon as this storm clears, we're headed your way for backup."

"Is that safe? What if he's watching Secure One?"

"Let me worry about us here while you do your job there. Keep Selina safe tonight. Eat. Get rest. Try to remember we're a team and we do better working with each other instead of against each other. We'll be in contact in the morning. Charlie, out."

Efren dropped the phone to his side and turned to stare out at the storm. The wind whipped and howled, and the sleet pelted down, changing direction with each turn of the wind. If his soul were an image, that would be it. This had become more than an assignment the moment he'd put his lips on hers. If they were going to get out of this alive, he was going to have to keep his head in the game. It was his job to convince Selina that this was one time the cops didn't need to be involved until after Secure One had gone in and doled out a bit of karma to the two people who deserved it most. After spending the last few days with her, he suspected it wouldn't be a hard sell. This was one time Selina Colvert might agree that manipulating fate was the right thing to do.

Chapter Fourteen

The stitches were out and Selina was feeling much better about life, even as a storm rolled around outside their tiny wooden structure, a madman and her twin were after her, and the man she was trapped with had flipped a switch and turned into king jerk of the universe. There was nothing she could do about the storm, the madman or Ava, but she could talk to the man who had switched into defense mode to protect himself. He'd helped her with the stitches begrudgingly, more than a little surprised when her skin was perfectly healed as she'd predicted.

What he didn't know was that her trained eye picked up the bounce he did every three or four steps on his blade as he paced the small room. That was something he didn't normally do. They'd decided to stay in the main room for as long as the heater stayed running. Eventually, they'd take turns sleeping and keeping watch until the storm passed and they could connect with the team again. In the meantime, she was going to have to convince him to let her look at his limb and treat any problems with it before they became major ones. Considering his attitude over the last few hours, she suspected that would be easier said than done.

Efren was dealing with some internal battle Selina wasn't privy to. She could see it in his body language and the way he set his jaw. What he couldn't control was the look in his coffee-brown eyes every time he glanced at her. Every so often, he'd run his hand through his short, curly hair and sigh. An hour ago, he'd moved the wardrobe away from the front door and gone outside. She could see he was talking on the sat phone, but he refused to answer any of her questions about why he had to call Secure One. He paced, huffed and sighed like the entire world was on his shoulders. Considering the circumstances, it was a real possibility that was how he felt as he sat trapped in a cabin with her. They both knew what was coming, and their war would likely include fatalities. They just had to hope those fatalities were on the enemy's side.

She'd call him out about his phone call later. For now, she had a bigger problem to solve. "Stop." She stood in front of him so he had no choice but to. "You have a situation with your leg. Sit down so I can look at it."

"My leg is fine." He growled the words more than he spoke them, and she lifted a brow.

She wasn't new to dealing with surly guys who didn't want to take the time to deal with an injury. "It's not fine. Every four steps you're doing an unusual bounce to take pressure off the anterior side of the socket. Now, would you like to sit down so I can check the skin or would you like to stand here and argue about whether or not you have a problem when you know you're going to lose the argument anyway? I'm good either way. I have nothing else to do."

Efren glared at her with his lips pursed and his eyes

flaming. "You need to understand that I'm not comfortable with that idea. Let it go."

"Not happening. I don't care if you're uncomfortable. You're going to be more uncomfortable when you can't walk and we need to run. Pretend I'm a nurse at the VA if you have to, but sit down and take your socket off."

"I can't pretend you're a nurse at the VA," he said between clenched teeth as she dragged him to the couch near the heater. It put off a bit of light, and she'd need it to find the problem and repair it.

"Why not? You don't think I have the chops to be a nurse at the VA?"

"Oh, you have the chops, but I'm far more interested in you as a woman than any nurse I've dealt with at the VA."

He sat and she knelt in front of him, zipping off his pant leg to turn them into shorts. It was Mack who had found creative ways to dress the crew, who all had different braces and prostheses to wear. These pants worked great for getting their clothes changed quickly without taking their devices off. No one realized what a pain that was until they no longer had to do it. She removed the valve in the prosthesis to release the suction and glanced up at him. "I can be both and separate myself as each. Take it off."

His sigh was heavy, but he finally grasped the socket and pulled, carefully working it back and forth until it was off and he could set it aside. Selina took in the limb as a whole. His skin bore the typical changes that came with wearing a skin-fit prosthesis for years. The scar at the distal end of the femur was well done and shaped the limb nicely, but there was an area where a sore had developed.

Selina glanced up at him. "There's a hell of a blister on the scar."

"Kind of figured," he said, grasping his thigh and rubbing it. "The longer I wear the blade, the worse the phantom pain gets, and that changes my gait."

"Yet you refuse to let me take care of it when I have the skills to do it. Someone told me you were smart." Rather than wait for a response, she grabbed the first aid kit from his bag, and a clean towel from the bathroom cabinet. They'd both showered, which wasn't easy for him, but he'd managed by using a kitchen chair to sit on. The fact that he showered, saw the problem and refused to do anything about it really jacked her pickles. "You could have a little respect for what I do at Secure One." She tossed him the towel in anger, and he caught it midair. "Do your massage while I work on the blister."

"What are you so peeved about? I'm out here trying to help you, and you're giving me attitude."

"I'm giving you attitude because you showered, saw the problem and still didn't ask for help!"

He slung the towel under his thigh and moved it back and forth in a pattern he'd mastered, while she readied the first aid supplies she'd need to treat the blister and keep it from getting bigger. "I don't like coming to you for help."

"Well, thanks for the vote of confidence." Her eye roll punctuated the sarcasm in the sentence.

"Not because you're incompetent, Selina." He grabbed her hand, and she glanced up at him. "I'm supposed to be the one protecting you. How do you have confidence in that when I show you my weakest link?"

"It's not your weakest link, Efren. This doesn't stop you." She motioned at his leg. "What stops you is this." She tapped her temple. "You overthink things instead of following your gut. You're the one whispering in my ear to follow mine. Why aren't you doing the same?"

"Following my gut would be a dangerous thing for you, Selina Colvert. If you were wise, you'd rethink telling me to do so."

"I can hold my own with you, Efren Brenna." Without waiting for his response, she inspected the scar while he held the limb up with the towel. The blister had already popped, which made the cleaning and bandaging easier, but they'd have to watch for infection until they could get back to Secure One.

"Mina said you were injured by an IED but saved six men that day?" It was time to change the subject before she told him how much she wanted him to follow his gut when it came to her.

"For what it was worth, yes," he agreed.

"Purple Heart?" She swiped antiseptic over the wound. His next words were hissed. "Yep, and Bronze Star."

"What does it feel like to be a hero? Like a real hero?"

"Don't be condescending, Selina." His words were cold, and she glanced up to meet his clouded gaze. Whether it was pain or anger clouding it, she couldn't be sure.

"I'm not, Efren. It's a sincere question."

"I could ask you the same thing. You did an awful lot of saving when you were Eva Shannon."

"Not like you. Not missing a limb and bleeding out

on the field. That's next-level stuff right there. Besides, I wasn't a hero. I was a cop doing my job, and in the case of search-and-rescue, that was something I enjoyed doing that benefited others. That's it."

"I'm sorry for being short, but you made my point. I don't like the word *hero*. It sets my teeth on edge."

"Because?" She wanted to keep him talking so he wouldn't notice what she was doing with his limb. Keeping his mind focused on something other than her messing with the sore would hopefully keep him from having worse phantom pain when she finished. The nervous system and mind were so closely connected that it was difficult for amputees to train their brains not to focus on the pain, which was understandable. Unfortunately, messing with his limb was going to make it worse for a few days.

"I don't believe in heroes. Heroes are people we inflate in our minds as being more than human, and that's not right. Did I save six men that day in the field? Yes. Are they all still here on this earth? No. Since returning that day, we've lost three—one to his injuries and two to the scars the event left on their mind."

"I'm sorry. That's a tough reality, considering you went through the same experiences."

"It is, which is why I agreed to be a bodyguard when the opportunity came my way. I could protect people in danger for any number of reasons and deliver them safely to the other side. Score another soul for Efren that he managed to keep on this earth, at least for a little while longer. I know it isn't a healthy way to deal with the aftermath of the war, but I haven't figured out any other way."

"I wouldn't say it's unhealthy." Her fingers deftly applied a special transparent skin to the limb, and she held it gently while it settled in. "There are much worse ways of dealing with it."

"I've seen those ways, too, and didn't want to go down that road. I thought going back over there as a contractor would be better. It would give me more power to help those people, but it didn't. If anything, it gave me less power. I didn't like it, so I came back stateside and started protecting witnesses and domestic abuse survivors. That's where I found satisfaction in using my skills to help others."

"Why Secure One, then?"

"I came running because Mina called. That was the only reason. Mina, Roman and I worked together quite frequently when they were FBI. As one of the main bodyguards for WITSEC witnesses, we did a lot of co-ordinating."

"Ah, that explains why you were so concerned I was part of the program." Selina lowered his limb to the couch for support and pulled off her gloves to clean up the mess.

"That explains why I was so surprised to find out you did this on your own. Most people struggle to do it with the government behind them. I could only imagine how hard it was without them."

"It was a struggle, but I always knew that one day I might have to run, so I had planned for the contingency in the way I lived my life."

"What was it like growing up with a dad who was part of the Mafia? What did your mom think about it?"

"My mother died in childbirth. I was born first, but

Ava was breech. They saved Ava, but my mother was gone. Dad named me Eva because it means life and her Ava because it means to live. My mother was Italian and her name was Bibiana, which meant full of life. Dad always said we carried her life. All of that said, he had no idea how to raise two baby girls, so he hired a nanny who cared for us until we were old enough to go to school."

"Your dad never remarried?"

"Thankfully, no. We found out shortly after he died that my parents had only been married eight months before we were born."

"A shotgun wedding?"

"Apparently, and not one based on love. Uncle Medardo had insisted he make an honest woman out of her. He wanted my father to play the part of the family man to bolster Medardo's attempt to change the face of the organization."

"Uncle?"

"That's what we called him growing up," Selina said with a shrug. "Looking back on it, it was weird, but we didn't know that he was a cold-blooded killer who used people like napkins and threw them away when he was done. Hell, we lived with a man who would kill on command."

"Did you know what your dad's job was? Seems like an odd thing to tell your kids."

"He didn't tell us. According to him, he was Uncle Medardo's business partner. I was twelve when I learned what he did for a living." She pointed at his socket. "Do you have pads you can put in there to protect that spot?"

"The small black bag in the front zipper. What happened when you were twelve?"

Selina walked to his go bag and knelt, pulling out the smaller supply bag and carrying it over to him. "I was supposed to wait in the car that night." She sat next to him and took his limb onto her lap, starting the towel massage so he could fix the socket. "He was taking forever and I was hungry. Since he'd gone into a pizzeria, I figured I'd run in, grab a snack and be back before he missed me."

"Instead?"

"Instead, I walked into the restaurant to see my father aiming a gun at a man who was on the ground groveling for his life. The man next to him already had a bullet between his eyes. My father said, this is done by order of the Snake, and then put a bullet between that guy's eyes. Thankfully, they were in a side room and my father never knew I was there. I got back in the car and waited for him like I hadn't just witnessed him kill someone. Intrinsically, I knew it would be dangerous to my life if I let on about what I saw, so instead, I spent six years plotting out a way to take him down when I got old enough. I saw police work as the only way, so as soon as I graduated from high school, I went to the academy. I had dreamed of one day being in the FBI, but I knew a dream was all it would ever be. What about you? Are your parents alive?"

"Yep, alive and well," he said as he added a pad to the socket. "My dad is from Italy, and my mom is from Bolivia. My dad worked for the UN, so I was born here in the States. They eventually became citizens when they retired."

"That explains the exotic skin tone," she said, running her hand up his forearm. "Mina always says you're the epitome of tall, dark and handsome."

"Do you agree?"

"It would be hard to disagree with that statement. Do you talk to your parents often?"

"Nice pivot, Colvert," he said, chuckling. "I talk to them every Sunday and keep them updated about where I am. I got a message to them while you were at the hospital that I was on a new case and didn't know when I'd call next. They've always been supportive of what I do, but they've enjoyed me working at Secure One. They like that I've found a way to do what I love and have a brotherhood again. They've seen how the loner lifestyle changed me, I suppose, and as parents do, they worry."

"Is that why you've stayed at Secure One? For the brotherhood?" Selina was trying to concentrate on doing the massage the way he did while they talked. It was her fault he was in this bind, so she would do what she could to give him some relief.

"That's one of the reasons I've stayed. It's refreshing to work with a team of people I trust where we're doing good things to help people. Even if we have to operate under the law a bit to do it."

"I try to avoid that," she said with a bit of a lip tilt. "Sometimes we can, sometimes we can't. When it came to Randall Jr., we couldn't. When it comes to the Snake, we will, and I fully support that."

His brows went up. "Seriously? You're okay with not bringing the cops in on this?"

"There's a certain finesse that will be needed on this case. No one knows that better than me. Is that what your little tête-à-tête was about out there? You could have talked to me about it before you went to Cal."

"I was going to, but I wanted his approval before I presented it as an option to you. It doesn't matter what our plans are if Cal's are different. He runs the show."

"True. We'll have to bring the cops in, but it can be after the fact."

"After what fact? After Ava and Vaccaro are dead?"

"If that's what has to happen," she answered. "Are you going to leave Secure One after this and go back to bodyguarding?"

His laughter was quiet as he shook his head. "We'll have to discuss the plan in further detail, but I'll let it go until morning when we meet with the team. As for what happens after this case, no, I'm not leaving Secure One." He finished with the socket and set the leg down. "Cal has hired me on full-time. He's starting the cybersecurity division now with Mina, and he needs a strong team for the rest of the security work. I'll be bodyguarding, but for Secure One instead of the government. It will be a tighter team when this op is over."

"What does that mean?" She paused with the towel, confused by his statement.

"It means that it's time for you to set your stethoscope aside and pick up your gun again. You proved yourself last week as an invaluable operative. If Cal wants me to stay, we're a package deal."

"You're going to quit if he doesn't move me to operations from medical?"

"Without a moment's hesitation. My goal in life is to right wrongs, and you're a wrong that Cal needs to make right. You have the training and the chops to do what all those other guys do, the only difference is, you're a woman. I would hope by now, Cal has seen the difference all the women who have joined Secure One have made to his business. If he doesn't, then I don't want to work for him."

"Despite how I've treated you?"

"Partly because of the way you treated me. It intrigued me. I wanted to know why you were so upset that I was there when the team so obviously needed help. I understand now." His finger traced her cheek, and the sensation sent a skitter of desire through her. "You didn't hate me. You hated what I represent."

"It wasn't fair to you." Her whispered admittance released a tightness in her chest she'd been carrying for too long. "I hated you for coming in and stealing my chance to take down the Red River Slayer."

"That's nonsense. I had nothing to do with that capture. I was there to guard the senator's daughter."

"But had they needed another person, they weren't going to pull the nurse off the injured woman, were they? No, they were going to go to the tall, dark and handsome stranger who had proven himself in the same war they'd fought."

"That's fair, and logical. Coupled with what you were dealing with as the caretaker of these women, I can understand the hostility you felt toward the newcomer. The Red River Slayer case has been over for almost a year. Why the continued animosity?"

"I'm always nervous when Cal brings someone new in. The Snake's reach is far and wide."

"I'm not a Vaccaro plant. I've only been to Chicago once."

"I know. And that's not why I've kept you at arm's length. There's this draw between us that's too hard to fight if I don't put up a wall." He gently pushed her hands aside and rolled on an elastic sock.

"That will control the nerves for now. As much as I love having your hands on me, I can't handle having your hands on me." He tugged her up onto the couch next to him and grasped her hands. "I feel the draw, too. Why do you want to fight it?"

Why did she want to fight it? That was a complicated answer to a simple question. "For starters, I'm a woman in a man's world."

"That's not the reason," he said, grasping her chin and forcing eye contact. "Mina is a woman in a man's world. So are Charlotte and Marlise."

"I'm not them." Her words were defensive. "I've had different life experiences. I don't know how to connect the way they do. Even if we wanted to explore this draw, I wouldn't know how."

"Wrong. You're scared. Just admit it, and then we can move on. We have to stop being afraid to be afraid. We have to stop letting the fear control us and use the fear to motivate us. Do you want me to admit it first? Okay. I'm scared of what this draw between us could mean. Every look, every interaction, every time I kiss you, it's a reminder that I can still feel. After I lost my leg and the men I cared about, I swore that I would never fall in love or have a long-term relationship. Life can change in an instant and someone you love can be taken just as quickly. Then I met you, and your attitude toward me hurt. Suddenly, I cared that you didn't like me even though you didn't know me. Those were dangerous feelings. I'm not supposed to care, but when it comes to you, I do. I care what you think about me, and I worry that this—" he motioned at his leg "—makes you think that I can't protect you as well as Roman or Cal could."

"No." The word was said quickly and with conviction. "I would trust you to protect me as much or more than I'd trust Cal or Roman."

"Why?"

"You've proved your mettle, Efren. You've kept me alive longer than I ever thought possible when Vaccaro entered our lives again. You haven't just kept me alive, but you've included me in the decisions that affect my life. That's more than anyone else at Secure One has done. You demand respect for yourself and the same respect for me. The only time the amputation is a factor is when you're limping and not taking care of yourself. That doesn't mean you can't protect me. You would lay down your life for me, which, while misguided, is the true definition of protection."

"Misguided? Why would dying for you be misguided?"

"Because no matter how much you give, you can't save me, Efren. You'd lay down your life and he'd slither right over you to get to me."

"Maybe you're right. Maybe I can't save you, but I can support you while you save yourself. You don't need a hero, Selina. You can fight Vaccaro and win as long as you have the right team behind you. Secure One is the right team. Every single one of your friends back home is busy making a plan to defend you. Find that woman inside you who stood on the top of a bluff and asked a man who loved her to support her one last time. Find the woman who survived and thrived on her own despite having the deck stacked against her. Let her guide you again, and the rest of us become soldiers in *your* army."

She was straddling him now to get closer. To be closer to the man who saw things in her that she didn't see in herself. "What if I want you to be more than a soldier?" Her question was soft as she lowered her head toward his, their noses touching as she waited for him to answer.

"I thought you were scared to be more with me."

"You told me to stop being afraid of being afraid. It sent me back to the woman who stood on a bluff and broke a man's heart in order to do the right thing. She used fear as motivation. Right now, that fear is motivating her to kiss you, Efren Brenna."

"Then she should quit talking about it—"

He didn't have a chance to finish the sentence before her lips were on his and the storm inside was stronger than the one knocking on their door.

Chapter Fifteen

"Selina, we have to stop," Efren said against her warm lips. Lord knew he didn't want to, but he also knew if he had this woman once, he'd want her every day for the rest of his life, and that was not in the cards for him.

Stop being afraid of being afraid.

He inhaled a breath, hating that voice for being right and being wrong at the same time. This wasn't being afraid of being afraid. This was protection. This was the way he protected himself from having to live in a world where his failures as a man and a soldier were always with him.

"We don't." Selina leaned back and took his face in her hands. "This connection between us has already been made. Trying to fight it will only be a lesson in frustration."

"Oh, trust me, I'm frustrated," he assured her, shifting under the sweet warmth of her draped across his lap. "That doesn't mean it's a good idea. Emotions complicate everything."

"You're right," she said, kissing the right side of his lips. "The biggest thing they complicate is our internal fight to protect our hearts from the pain of losing someone. It's an unfortunate side effect of the jobs we've done in the past. Those memories stay with us and shape every decision we make in the future. If we let them." She whispered the final sentence in his ear, and it sent a shiver of anticipation, expectation and desire down his spine. "How long are we going to give it that power before we pull it back and control our future again?"

"Up until a year ago, I'd planned to give it the power for the rest of my life. Tonight, here with you on my lap, I'm rethinking that plan."

"I bet I can make you rethink it quicker," She lifted a brow, and it transformed her from the beautiful woman she was to a sexy vixen whom he wanted to make love to for the rest of his life. Selina slipped her hand between them and caressed his undeniable source of frustration.

He grasped her face and attacked her lips, thrusting against her hand while he searched for relief from the sweet torture she doled out. "Let me put my leg on," he said against her lips. "We'll go to the bedroom."

She leaned out of the kiss and lifted herself on her knees. Her shirt came off in a slow striptease, offering a full frontal that turned him on and hurt him at the same time. He traced the scars that marred her skin while he held her eye. It wasn't until his hands moved toward the clasp on her bra that she spoke. "We're not going to the bedroom. I want to make love to you right here, being open and honest with each other with all of our scars visible. These scars are part of us and will remain that way forever. I accept yours, Efren. Do you accept mine?"

He didn't answer with words. He deftly twisted her until she was on her back on the small sofa and he was kissing every scar across her belly, his featherlight touch raising goose bumps across her bare skin as he moved farther north. It wasn't until those kisses landed on her nipples that she inhaled deeply. "Efren, make me yours. Now."

Her words shot fire through him, and he finished relieving them of their clothes until every painful scar and emotion was laid bare. "I have to grab some protection," he whispered as he kissed his way up the inside of her thigh.

"We don't need any."

The way she said it made him lift his head to meet her gaze. Her eyes were open and honest, and he chastised himself for forgetting something so important in the moment. He slid alongside her until he was able to kiss her lips. "I'm sorry. I forgot. Can we even do this? It hasn't been that long since your surgery."

"I'm fine," she assured him, running her hand through his hair. "I just want to feel something other than scared tonight. I'm not afraid of being with you anymore. I have no control over the storm outside, but I have control of the one inside me. That storm says only you can calm it, but first, you're going to have to fight through the waves threatening to take you under."

"I'm not afraid of those waves," he promised, scooting back on the couch and lifting her gently by her waist to sit across him. "Let's dive in and let them take us under together."

Selina leaned forward and took his lips with hers, kissing him senseless while her warmth settled around him. It was a moment before the sensation broke through the high he was on from holding her sweet body. When it did, he thrust upward with a moan nearly as loud as the ones from the storm outside.

"Selina," he hissed, thrusting his hips against hers until they were locked together in harmony and ecstasy.

She leaned back and braced herself on his thigh, taking him under the waves for a moment before she brought him back up, setting him on top to savor the pleasure. She paused, their heightened senses meshing as they entangled their hands and rode out the storm. With a satisfied sigh, they rested together in the calmness of their connection.

SELINA PACED THE small cabin as she tried to put together in her mind a way to make Vaccaro and Ava disappear from her life. She paused near the couch where the man she'd made love to three times in the same number of hours now rested. She'd insisted he catch a nap since she knew she wouldn't sleep. She was energized by the great sex but riddled with anxiety about what was to come—both with Vaccaro and her life now that she'd admitted she cared for Efren.

Stop being afraid of being afraid.

Those six words echoed through her head as she kept an eye on the perimeter of the cabin. The lesson she took from those words was to live life afraid. Playing it safe means the only winner is fear. In this case, playing it safe with Vaccaro meant he would be the winner in this decades-long game of cat and mouse. Playing it safe with Efren meant they'd both lose. They were good together, both as work partners and as life partners.

"Life partners?" she muttered. Back up the wagon. They shared some secrets and made love—no, they had sex three times. Not the definition of life partners. The question she kept trying to block from her mind—the one where the answer made her afraid—was, could they be life partners given a little more time and trust?

She was afraid because the answer, at least for her, was yes. She had always had feelings for Efren that went beyond basic colleagues. This night made their lives so much more complicated, especially considering she was still being hunted by a madwoman with an axe to grind. And she had no doubt they were still being hunted. This little interlude had been too good to be true, and as soon as the sun came up in a few hours, a memory was all it would be. A memory was all it would ever be if she didn't figure out a way to get Vaccaro and Ava off her back and keep Randall Sr. in prison.

Selina's heart pounded hard in her chest at the thoughts running through her head. If she could get that witness statement signed before Randall went before the judge, she might be able to keep him in prison. Efren's words came back to her then, and her shoulders slumped. He was right. Even if she did get the statement signed, if Vaccaro had already paid off the judge, she was risking her life for nothing. There had to be a better way.

Fear was keeping her from thinking through the better way. The fear she'd carried for so long wanted her to run back to Secure One and hide behind the fortress while someone else fought her battles. The other side of the fear told her she'd done that long enough. It was time she stepped up and took control of her own destiny again. When she was Eva Shannon, she was the kind of person who didn't hesitate when a decision had to be made, fear or no fear. She faced the fear head-on in her job so many times that it had simply become how she lived her life until her entire life became a calculated risk.

Selina had spent too long not taking any risks, calculated or otherwise. That, she realized, was why she hadn't pushed Cal to make her part of the core team as something other than medical. While she was mad about it, she was also afraid to rock the boat. If Cal did make her part of the team, then the safety she'd found in the med bay would be gone. She'd have to expose herself to the outside world again. Her life had become a yin-yang that she couldn't break. She wanted something she couldn't have but didn't want what she already had.

Selina recalled the woman who stood on that bluff eight years ago. That woman had an actionable plan that put her in complete control. That woman wasn't afraid to ask for everything from someone when she couldn't repay him. That woman was not afraid of the fear that engulfed her because the fear kept her alive.

She paused and gazed at Efren, his hair tousled in sleep and a deep five-o'clock shadow covering his chin. She wanted him more than any man she'd wanted in her lifetime. Fear rocketed through her at the idea of asking someone to be part of her life when her life was always a calculated risk. She'd let fear stop her from asking Kai. She couldn't make the same mistake with Efren, right? They had survived bombs, bullets and pain to get here. Those bombs and bullets didn't take their lives, which meant they shouldn't let them take their future.

Determined to get her life back, she grabbed a notebook and pen, then stood to the side of the window to use the light of the moon to write. The storm had blown out of town about an hour ago, and as happened in Minnesota, the sky cleared off immediately, dropping the temps to a teeth-chattering cold. The rain and sleet that had fallen was surely going to freeze, turning everything into an ice-skating rink until the sun came out to melt it. They'd have to be extra careful when they left the cabin so Efren didn't slip. His limb was already in rough shape, and falling could mean life or death for them. Thankfully, he had his spiked sole and his all-terrain sole with him.

What was that sound? Her brain registered it and dropped her to the floor under the window. She crab-walked to the other side of the cabin to peer out the window on that side from under the curtain. Her fear had been confirmed. A drone hovered around the yard, obviously trying to get a look inside the cabin. They had turned the propane heater off and with no lights on, as long as they stayed low, the drone would show its pilot nothing but an empty cabin.

Still in a crouch, Selina moved to the couch and put her hand on Efren's chest from where she sat on the ground. His eyes opened immediately and met hers. "Drone," she mouthed, and he slid off the couch onto the floor, curling himself around her as they listened for the faint sound of the flying spy to disappear—if it disappeared.

"How did they find us?" he whispered into her ear.

"Vaccaro has eyes everywhere, but this is a stretch even for me. We've left no digital trail and made no purchases."

"That's not entirely true," Efren whispered. "The sat phone leaves a digital trail when it goes to the service provider for billing, but Cal assured me it was safe to use."

"Nothing and no one is safe from Vaccaro. You used the phone what, five hours ago? They already found us. I'm surprised all we have is a drone in the air and not ten guys knocking down the door."

"Only because a satellite phone can't pinpoint where the call is coming from. It will give them a quadrant to search, so they know we are in the area, but they don't know our precise location. Using a drone makes sense. As soon as it's gone, so are we."

"To where?" Selina asked, rolling over to make eye contact.

"Anywhere but here. We need to get free of this place and then get connected with the team. I'm done letting this idiot control our lives."

"Me, too," she whispered with a nod. "I have a plan, but it's going to require backup from Secure One and a dance with a devil who's the spitting image of me."

"Wrong," he hissed, slamming his lips into hers to quiet them. "You may be identical twins, but that woman wears her evil like a fine linen cloak. You're like night and day. Remember, your fear feeds the devil, but if you stay strong, you'll starve her for good."

"That's where you're wrong," she whispered. "The devil gets her power from a snake, but once we've shredded his scaly body and buried him ten feet deep, the devil will become mortal once again. I no longer fear Ava or Vaccaro. I fear giving up another second of my life to them. Eva Shannon may be dead, but before she went over that cliff, she transferred her power to Selina Colvert. The time to bide is over. The time to do is upon us." She paused and they listened, but the night was silent again. "Are you ready to act rather than react?"

He pushed himself up and then held out his hand for her. "Secure one, Tango."

Selina slid her palm into his and let him pull her up. "Secure two, Sierra."

Quickly, they dressed for the weather and readied their bags. Selina held up a fist at the door of the cabin and they listened for several moments, but heard nothing but silence. "When we get out there, follow me and don't ask questions."

"Ten-four."

Efren pressed against her back, but she paused. "Ten-four? No arguments?"

"I knew from the moment I met you that I'd follow you anywhere, Sierra."

A ghost of a smile played on her lips as she opened the door. Today was the day she took her life back.

Chapter Sixteen

The night was as cold as Efren was expecting it to be, but he'd stayed close on Selina's heels, his gun out and his head on a swivel as they worked their way downstream, following the river. She had a plan, so he was going to let her lead until she asked for help. Selina didn't need anyone to save her. She could save herself as soon as she channeled the woman she'd hidden away so many years ago. That must have happened during the hour he'd been asleep, because the woman leading him now was completely different than the one he'd known over the last year.

Then again, as he thought about it, he'd been watching it happen over the course of the last week. Slowly, she was coming to realize that waiting around for someone else to help her out of this jam wasn't the answer. If she wanted to be free of Ava and Vaccaro, she was going to have to do the saving herself, even if it scared her.

And it scared her.

He could see it in her eyes when the drone was flying over their heads, but she hadn't buckled to the fear. She'd used it to spur her forward, and something told him she was just getting started. Their lovemaking came back to him, and he couldn't help but smile, even as they trudged along the cold, wet banks of the Mississippi. He loved nothing more than when a woman was willing to dominate him in the bedroom. Did he always allow it? No, but last night, he sensed that it was a first step for Selina to be in control again, and he was all too happy to give her that power. She deserved it. She harnessed it, and now she would use it to find her twin and put an end to this game of hide and seek.

For him, the most challenging part would be to put the image of her sweet, hot body on top of his out of his mind long enough to help her get the job done. Especially since the things his body told him about his time with her confused his mind and heart. Selina deserved a better life than she'd lived the last decade, but that didn't mean he could be the one to give her that life. Damn if he didn't want to, though. He couldn't remember the last time someone turned him on with a lifted brow and a snide remark, but Selina did every time.

His body contracted at the memories of the way she turned him on. His mind was blown at the number of times he'd made love to her last night and still couldn't get enough of her. He wanted her now. Cold, tired, hungry and sore, he'd still lay her down on the beach and frolic in the sand with her.

"Almost there," she whispered through a huffed breath as they hurried through the woods.

"Almost where?" He hoped she knew where she was going, because he was utterly lost. They'd been running parallel to the river, but other than that, it looked like trees and not much else.

"We need to get somewhere safe to call into Secure

One before daybreak. We can't risk turning on the emergency tracking beacon, even if Cal says it's hidden from everyone but him. Vaccaro has bested us at every turn."

Selina was right, and Efren ran the crew at Secure One through his mind, looking for a mole. Their newest hire, Sadie Cook, had suffered at the hands of the Loraines, which was what prompted all of this just a few weeks ago, so there was no way it was her. He made a mental note to suggest to Cal that he check his people again. Efren hadn't been at Secure One long enough to know everyone well, but if there was a Vaccaro mole in play, Cal would find them.

"That drone could still be out here," he whispered as they pulled up to a tree and stopped. Selina leaned over to give her side a break and take a breather. He rubbed her back, hoping to relieve some tension there from the injury she was still dealing with despite her rapid improvement. "I haven't heard it again, though, so Vaccaro doesn't have a lock on us yet. My gut says that could still change."

"That's why we moved as fast as we did," she agreed. "We couldn't get picked up by their drone, but I also didn't want to miss our ride out of here."

"Our ride out of here?"

After straightening again and doing a bit of a side stretch, she pointed at the area in front of them that was still pitch black. "What time is it?"

He flipped his wrist to check his watch. "It's 4:37. Daybreak will be coming soon."

"So will our ride."

"Did you hire a rescue chariot? Because all I see is darkness."

"What you don't see are the train tracks in front of us," she whispered with a satisfied glint in her eye. "There will be a train coming along in the next few minutes. It's our ticket out of town."

Efren slid his hand into hers and turned her to face him. "We can't jump a train, Selina. That's crazy dangerous. I've already lost a leg. I can't afford to lose an arm, too."

"Why do you think I picked this spot? We could have picked up the tracks not too far from the cabin, but the train would be going too fast. By the time the train gets to this part of the track, it's slowing for a junction ahead. Your grandma could get on it at that point, so jumping the train will be safe and easy. Finding an open boxcar will be harder. Worst case, we take the stairs on the caboose, but that will leave us open to sight once the sun comes up."

"How do you know all this? We don't even know exactly where we are."

"Last night, while you were sleeping, I heard a whistle off in the distance. Mina said we were north of Winona, so that meant there was a cargo train moving through the area. All I had to do was be here when one went by. Luckily, we won't have to wait long. I'll have to thank Vaccaro when I see him for sending that drone up and getting us out the door early."

"How do you know all of this?" he asked as she kept her head turned up the track.

When she turned back, she wore a sad smile. "This is my old stomping grounds for search-and-rescue, Efren. We did a lot of work on the Mississippi and the surrounding areas. The bluffs near La Crosse are just downriver from here a bit."

"Are those the bluffs you—"

"No," she said with a shake of her head, already knowing what he was thinking. "But it's the same type of topography. Being here, it makes me nostalgic for those days and the days I used to spend with Zeus and Kai tracking the lost and wounded. On the other side of the coin, it makes me angry that Vaccaro stole my passion and turned me into someone else entirely."

"That's not true," he said, stepping up and taking her face in his hands. "You're still the same caring person who wants to rescue others. You just do it in a different way now."

Her head tipped in his hands, and her beautiful navy blue eyes turned confused. "I put Band-Aids on scrapes and hydrate grown men who push themselves too far?"

"You also nursed hurt and scared women back to health to the point that they can now lead healthy, happy lives with a man, which is a testament to the care they got at Secure One. Just a few weeks ago you took on the role of caregiver again when you took care of a scared baby and his aunt, while terrified of the man after them, I may add. Then you set the fear aside and stepped up with the information the team needed to prepare for a mission. A mission you went on to rescue two people in danger where you paid heavily. If that weren't enough, over the last year, week and last night, you rescued me." He leaned in to kiss her softly without lingering, but did allow his thumb to keep caressing her temple.

"Rescued you from what?"

"The need to be everyone's savior. The self-hatred I

carried about the men I've lost since returning to friendly soil. The fear that I would never be enough for anyone and the loneliness I've been drowning in for years."

"My catty attitude toward you did all of that?" She tipped her head up to make eye contact, and he saw the truth in her eyes. She needed to know that he didn't hold any of that against her.

He hoped what she saw there was more than his words could convey. "It did, sweetheart. That attitude set an ember burning in my chest again. It gave me a reason to fight when I no longer had the spirit. This past week, when you've put your trust in me to keep you safe, it reminded me that I can still do the job. Last night, when you put your trust in me as a woman, it reminded me that I still have something to offer the right person, even if we come from different experiences in life." She gazed at him, as though she was unsure what to say, so he dropped a soft kiss on her lips and then tipped his head upstream. "I think I hear the train."

That sentence snapped her out of her trance, and she whipped her head to the right, listening for a moment before she nodded. "It's coming. We need to get in position, which means still in the trees, but once the conductor is past, we get as close to the cars as we can. As soon as we see a workable situation, we go for it."

"The conductor won't see us?"

"Not in the dark and on his flank." She moved to the edge of the trees and flipped down her night-vision goggles. "You with me, Tango?"

After flipping his goggles down, he nodded with a smile. "Right behind you, Sierra."

Somewhere between the time the train passed and the

time he followed her onto an empty train car, he knew he'd always be behind her, rooting for her, and probably, if he were honest, loving her, even if from afar.

THE TRAIN RIDE had been slow, but Selina was happy for a chance to sit down and give her side a break. It was healing, but her stamina was minimal, which meant pushing herself when all her body wanted to do was rest. Preferably rest in bed with the man who had held her during the train trip so she could lean against his chest and be comfortable.

Physically, she'd been comfortable, but emotionally, she'd been fighting against the things he'd said to her in the dark woods. His words made her rethink her place at Secure One again and what she wanted when this mission was over. Then again, wanting and getting were two entirely different words in the English language; no matter what she wanted, she would get what Vaccaro wanted her to have and nothing more. Unless they could take him and Ava down, she'd only get another ticket to run.

Selina shook off those thoughts and hung her legs over the edge of the doorway, motioning for Efren to do the same. "As soon as it starts to slow a bit more, push yourself off, drop and roll. Don't try to land on your feet."

"Got it, boss," he said, readying his hands to copy hers.

Jumping on and off trains was dangerous business that no one should be doing, but when it was a matter of living another day or falling into the Snake's hands, she'd take her chances with the train. At least she could walk away from the train with her life and limbs. The same couldn't be said of the Snake. She felt the slowing of the train under her and glanced at Efren. "See that opening in the trees?" Her finger swung out to the right, and he nodded. "Let's aim for that."

"You jump first. I'll follow once you land. That way, we won't land on each other."

Her nod was quick as she scooted to the edge, waiting for the right moment. Selina had no doubt that sticking this landing would hurt, but landing in the Snake's den would hurt worse. With a deep breath in, she pushed off the car, being sure to land on her right side, not that it mattered much when the hard earth smacked her ribs and sent a ricochet of pain through her entire body. Her momentum rolled her once before her backpack stopped her on the second roll. Selina scrambled to her feet, barely breathing, and ran for the opening in the woods as she watched Efren do the same from his southern position.

"You okay?" he asked as soon as he'd joined her, grasping her elbows to steady her. "I saw you land pretty hard on your side."

"There wasn't a choice, but I'm fine," she said between hissed breaths as she tried to make that statement true. "How's your leg?"

"Better than your side." He was eyeing her closely, probably trying to decide if he needed to carry her.

She forced herself to stand straight and then stretched side to side, trying to work out any last cramps from the fall and to keep new ones from starting. "We missed our check-in time with Secure One. It couldn't be helped, but we need to call in."

"Using the sat phone means another pin of our location for Vaccaro."

"Do we have a choice?" she asked, pulling the phone from her bag. "Last time it took him five hours to get the info. We'll be long gone in five hours."

When the screen came alive, Selina turned it so Efren could read the message. "Shady Lakes Campground. Number 117. ASAP. How are we supposed to know where that is? We don't even know where we are right now."

"You don't, but I do, and Cal knows it." Selina lowered the phone, but she couldn't keep her hand from shaking. Twisting to face south, she pointed to her left. "Ahead half a klick is the marina near Brownsville, which means we're about four klicks from the campground."

Without another word, Selina took off through the woods, knowing he would follow her without question. She had her compass out, following it south and then jogging west, praying her stamina held long enough to get to the campground. A mile and a half in, she slowed to a walk, bending over to catch her breath while Efren came up behind her, rubbing her side the way he did when she was hurting. Before she could speak, he relieved her of the backpack and carefully slipped his hand under her jacket to massage her side until the cramping eased.

"You gotta take it easy, sweetheart," he whispered in her ear. "This is a marathon, not a sprint."

"I know," she said, her breath still coming in spurts. "But the sooner we can link up with the team, the better. Wasting time because I'm weak could be a death sentence." She kicked the ground in front of her in frustration.

Efren wrapped his arms all the way around her and held

her to him. "You're not weak. A weak person wouldn't have jumped a train, jumped off a train and then run for two miles without stopping. You're recovering. You're not weak. There's a difference. Now, before we go any farther, are you familiar with the campground?"

"I've been there a few times for search-and-rescue, and it's a mix of modern and remote. The number he gave us is remote. We can bypass the campground through the woods and come at the site from the back side."

"When you're ready and at your pace," he said, releasing her, but slinging her backpack over his shoulders.

He would lighten the burden for her any way he could. She offered him a smile and then took off again, at a slower pace, not wanting to go too far past the campground. She was running blind without the convenience of a map or GPS, so she had to use her memory of her past to guide her. Those were painful. Those memories conjured the face of the man she'd left behind and the companion who had loved her unconditionally and understood her completely. How she had missed them both.

Memories of last night played through her mind, and she couldn't help but smile. She couldn't live in the past. She could only learn from it. She made a vow to herself right there as she slowed, sidestepping toward the edge of the trees and motioning for Efren to follow, that she'd take her life back. She'd find a way to be Selina Colvert and Eva Shannon for the benefit of others again.

She waved her hand at her throat as Efren stepped up to her. "That's 117, but it's empty. Did they leave?"

"Not without sending another coordinate," Efren answered, his eyes firing all around them. "The hair on the back of my neck is standing up, though, so we need to make a decision."

With clarity comes wisdom. That was a line Kai always said when they couldn't find their target on searches. "With clarity comes wisdom," Selina whispered. "Watch my back."

Before he could stop her, she broke through the brush and jogged to the wooden sign that said 117. She felt the thin ledge under it near the stake it was attached to. Sure enough, there was a piece of paper waiting. She grabbed it and ran back to Efren, who had his gun out and was sweeping the woods intently. Something had him spooked. He held his finger to his lips and waved his hand at his throat as he pointed at the note, then motioned for her to go south again.

She read the note as she pulled her gun from her holster and started forward. One klick west. That was it. Something told her getting one klick west was going to be hard won.

Chapter Seventeen

There had to be a mole in Secure One. Nothing else made sense. Efren motioned for Selina to move behind a tree, where they paused, listening for footsteps. If there wasn't a mole, then Vaccaro had a beacon on their location without Cal's knowledge. Considering the lengths Cal went to in order to ensure their security, that was saying something. Then again, if you ran a large crime organization, it was doubtful anyone could keep you from getting what you needed in a timely manner.

"What did the note say?" The whisper into her ear was barely audible.

She didn't speak; she held up one finger and then three. He nodded. One klick west. That wasn't far, unless they were ambushed on the way, and the hair on the back of his neck said that was a real possibility.

He leaned in closer again, keeping his gun pointed forward. "They're breaking through Cal's security layers. We can't lead them to Cal's front door."

"We can't have a gunfight this close to the campground," she hissed. "Too many civilians."

"I'm afraid that choice may not be ours. Let's move southwest and see what develops. Stay close. We don't

Katie Mettner 167

have the big guns." Selina glanced down at her hand-gun and grimaced, which was exactly how he felt. The bad guys had the big guns this time, and they were at a deadly disadvantage.

They hadn't made it ten steps when motion caught his eye. "Behind you!" They yelled in unison, both swinging around on instinct with their guns, right into a hulking body in black.

Efren threw a punch blindly, hoping to connect with the assailant who had knocked his gun away already. His fist glanced off the guy's shoulder but when he brought his knee up, it landed square in the nether regions. The guy grunted and doubled over, stunned long enough for Efren to finish him off with a hit to the trachea. The dude dropped and Efren recovered his gun and rolled, coming up in the shooter's stance, searching for Selina. A grunt whipped his head around and he saw Selina stumble backward as the guy pummeled her in the kidneys, rendering her motionless. She couldn't take much more, so he waited for her to drop to the ground and then fired off one perfectly placed round. The guy spun like a ballerina before he dropped like a rock, his carotid emptying his lifeblood onto the ground.

"Selina!" Efren whisper-yelled, scrambling to the woman who was now writhing on the ground. On his way, he scooped up her weapon and grabbed her by her jacket, pulling her behind a tree. "Talk to me, baby." He knelt over her, his lips near her ear as he waited for her to breathe normally again.

"I'm okay." The words were huffed, and he knew she wasn't okay, but she would be. "I'm real sick and tired of these guys popping up like Whac-A-Moles."

He smiled. Yeah, she was going to be fine. "Can you sit up? Lean against the tree for support." He helped her into a seated position, but his gaze darted around the woods, searching for more goons. "We will have to move as soon as you're able. There could be more out there."

"Two or four but never more," she recited as she rubbed at her side with a grimace. "Uncle Medardo used to say that to my father all the time. Dad told us it was a rule about nails and how many go in a board. How dumb was I?"

"You weren't dumb," he whispered with half a chuckle. "You were a kid. The theory being more than four leaves room for capture?"

"That's my assumption," Selina said, pushing herself up when they heard a pop.

They dropped, both waiting for a bullet to slam into one of them or a tree above their heads, but there was nothing. Efren glanced at Selina and motioned her to him, just as another pop reached their ears, followed by a growly moan.

"Secure one, Echo."

Efren let out the breath he was holding and stood. "Secure two, Tango."

"Secure three, Charlie," Cal said as he broke through the trees, dragging someone behind him. "Welcome back. Good to see you. We were getting a little worried." He tossed the guy in front of their feet and knelt. "This can go one of two ways," Cal told him. "I can finish you off and leave your corpse to rot in the woods, or you can tell me how many more of you undertrained, uneducated, technology-reliant infants are out here, and I'll give you a fighting chance with that gut wound."

Efren noted the guy was barely old enough to drink and the color of paste. Cal better get him to talk fast, because he had no fighting chance against that gut wound. Hopefully the kid didn't realize that yet.

"If I talk, I die," he murmured.

"The Snake has his ways, right?" Cal asked, turning chummy with the kid. "You just follow orders and keep your head down so you aren't the next target. How'd you get tied up with this jackass anyway? You seem like a nice kid."

Efren couldn't help but snicker, willingly playing along with Cal's technique. "Did you just call the kingpin of Chicago's Mafia a jackass?"

"If the shoe fits," Cal answered without looking at him.

"Vaccaro wants her," the kid said, lifting his arm to point at Selina. "The first guy to bring her to him gets promoted."

"Promoted?" Cal said, acting impressed. "To what? Head henchman?"

"Something like that," he said with a groan.

"That doesn't answer my question. How many more are coming?"

"If we don't come back, another team will follow, and another. It's impossible to escape the Snake once you're in his sights."

"That's true," Selina said, crouching beside the kid. "How about if I save you all the trouble and turn myself over to the Snake?"

"Only if you want to die, Eva," he said, spittle and blood starting to bubble up from his lips. "That's your real name, right? Your sister is good and tight with the

Snake now, if you know what I mean." He turned his head and spit, more blood bubbling up as he did so. Efren saw the moment he realized he was dying. There was no fear, just resignation. "I don't know who you all are, but if I were you," he said, pointing at Selina, "I'd run as fast and as far as you can, and I would have left ten minutes ago." He coughed, blood flowing freely from his lips as it also flowed over his hands, holding his stomach. "The next round will reach this location in thirty minutes. Less once I hit this." His bloody hand reached for his vest, but Eric stepped down on his stomach wound, stopping the guy cold.

"But you're not going to hit that," Eric said, his tone cold, hard and angry.

Cal searched the guy and found a beacon that he carefully unhooked from the vest.

"How many were there?" Selina asked, motioning toward the woods with her head.

"Two. The other guy is taking a dirt nap for eternity."

"Same for us," Efren said, motioning at the guys on the ground.

"We need to move," Cal said. "But first." He handed the beacon to Eric. "Get the rest of them and set them off somewhere before you double back."

Selina pointed upstream and to the right. "About a quarter mile back, a creek runs east toward the river. Toss them in there. It will buy us some more time."

With a nod, Eric disappeared into the trees like a ghost. Laughter bubbled up from the kid on the ground, though weak. "Tag, you're it. Run, run as fast as you can, sweet Eva…"

His words trailed off as his head lolled to the side,

his eyes staring blankly at the ground. Efren shuddered and looked away. "That's the second guy to say the exact same thing as he was dying."

"This is a game to Vaccaro," Selina said, holstering her gun. "It's the same thing Randall said to me the night I shot Ava eight years ago. Vaccaro makes the game rules, and he expects everyone to play."

"Well," Cal said as he started forward. "I don't know about you, but I'm not in the mood to play games with this idiot. I'd rather end his reign of terror the good old-fashioned way."

"With a bullet or brawn?" Efren asked as they hurried along behind him.

"First with brains, then brawn, but a bullet if necessary."

"Trust me," Selina huffed. "A bullet will be necessary."

CAL PULLED THEM up short near a gravel driveway. He reached for his phone, but Selina noticed Efren stop him. "Somehow, he knows your every move. Either you have a Vaccaro mole in Secure One or he has a mole in your communications company."

Cal sighed and shook his head. "I reran specs on all my people, and no one has connections to him other than Sadie and Selina, which we already knew. The communications company? Really?"

"I made that call to you last night on the sat phone and five hours later a drone was hovering over our cabin. You sent us the coordinates for the campground and an hour later, guys are in the woods looking for us."

"Damn it. Someone is inside my carrier, and they're supposed to be the best."

"The Snake's tentacles are many and wide," Selina said. "If you owe him a debt, you repay it when he comes to you. If you don't, you're dead. Even if you do, you're dead. As soon as you're no longer useful to him, he'll make sure you find a way out of his life for good."

"Comms are out then," Cal said with a shake of his head. "We'll have to use burner phones. I hate to do it, but by the time he figures out what we're doing by not using the carrier, we'll be knocking on his front door."

As they crept up the driveway, Selina was glad he'd had the forethought to bring burners with him, but then again, if he had mobile command, they had everything they'd need at their fingertips.

She had never been happier to see her friends show up when they did. If they hadn't, it would have been a dangerous endeavor to take on four guys by themselves. Especially worrying about civilian injuries if bullets started flying. The moment Cal tossed the guy down in front of them, dread filled her. People were dying, and her friends were going to be next if she didn't do something.

Her spine stiffened as she went back over the plan that she'd prepared this morning. She would have to stand her ground and force them to listen to her if they were going to come out of this alive as a team.

"Roman and Mina are waiting for us at mobile command," Cal said as he grabbed his birdcall from his pocket. He brought it to his lips and blew until a clicking, almost drumlike, sound filled the air.

A shudder went through Efren, and she stepped up against his back. "You okay?"

"Yeah," he whispered, shaking his head a bit. "The call of the white stork sends me back to the sandbox every time. It's how we called to each other since there were so many storks there. That's the first time I've heard it since I left."

Cal pocketed the birdcall and held their position, waiting and watching until they heard, "Secure one, Romeo."

"Secure two, Charlie," Cal answered, and Roman stepped out of the brush.

"It's good to see you guys," he said, shaking Efren's hand before he hugged Selina to his side. "Where's Echo?"

"He's running some interference for us."

"Why the birdcall?" Roman asked as they walked up the driveway, keeping an eye on both sides.

"Vaccaro has compromised our comms. I'll explain once we're inside."

When the vehicle came into view, Selina started. "This is new." The RV was white and had a rental company logo all over it.

"It's less conspicuous than mobile command," Cal explained. "I couldn't roll into town in that and expect Vaccaro not to notice. That's why it's tucked back here on private property. It's rented, so let's avoid putting any bullet holes in it."

They climbed the stairs and instantly, Mina was running toward them, grabbing Selina in a bear hug. "I'm so glad you're here. I've been worried sick about you guys."

"We're fine, Mina," Selina promised before she released her from the hug.

Mina eyed her carefully. "You don't look fine. You've got a bruise on your jaw and a black eye. Oh, wait, don't forget the busted lip."

Selina touched her lip and grimaced. "Better than getting punched in the gut." That was her only response.

When Selina glanced at Efren, she noticed he'd received the same treatment from their friends in the woods. His beautifully sculpted face now sported a black eye and a bruise across his nose. She'd have to check that it wasn't broken.

"Those guys aren't going to bother us again," Cal said, stripping off a few layers of clothes. "We do have a problem, Mina. Our comms are compromised."

Mina lifted her brow. "By Vaccaro?"

Cal motioned to Efren, who filled Mina in on what they'd experienced the last few days.

"That's not good," Mina said, her hand in her hair. "No wonder they could find us so easily. Burner phones?"

"Yep," Cal answered. "We'll use a burner phone app."

"A burner phone app on a burner phone?" Roman asked, digging out a bucket from under the table.

"A double layer of protection by using numbers that go away each time we make a call or send a text," Cal explained. "Best we can do under the circumstances."

Roman jumped up and ran for the door. "Eric doesn't know not to use comms," he said halfway out the door. "I'll find him and be back."

He was out the door and Mina was already shutting off her phones and equipment in a mad hurry. "This is going to cramp my style," she muttered. "It's going to be hard to track you guys with burner phones."

"You won't have to," Selina said, stepping toward Cal. "I have a plan. If we follow it to a T, most of us come out of this alive and unhurt. I will lay it out, but first, I need to tend to our injuries and address his leg."

"Everyone will come out of this alive and unhurt,"

Efren ground out, his eyes flaming when he looked at her. "Most especially you."

Mina raised a brow, but Selina ignored it. She didn't have time to argue with them. She'd lay out her plan, convince them it was the best way and then divert at the last minute. Sacrificing her life was worth it if it meant Secure One could continue to help people when this was finally over. They had their mission, and she had hers. As she walked to the back of the RV with Efren, his hand sitting naturally in hers, Selina knew the hardest part of the mission would be coming to terms with never feeling his touch again. It was just another item on her long list of things she hated Uncle Medardo for—a list she'd been keeping for twenty-three years. Now it was time to face the man, read him the list of sins and let him atone for them one bullet at a time.

Chapter Eighteen

Efren pulled Mina aside after Selina had set his broken nose and added a couple of butterfly bandages to his cheekbone. He probably needed stitches, but he wasn't interested in taking the time to do that right now. The rest of the team was preparing for battle, while he was preparing not to lose the woman he'd come to care about.

"Have you heard anything more about Daddy Dearest? Is the hearing still scheduled for tomorrow?"

"It is, but it won't be an in-person judgment."

"I don't understand."

"Randall will remain at the penitentiary and be connected via closed-circuit television. The prosecution is afraid that taking him out of prison for the judgment puts too many people at risk."

"They're naive enough to think that the judgment will go their way?"

Mina shrugged. "I can't tell you what they're thinking, only what they're doing."

"If the judgment goes his way, when will he be released?"

"The following day," Mina answered. "There's paperwork to be done and filed before he can be released."

pulling her to him by her coat and planting his lips on hers in a kiss he hoped would remind her why she wanted to.

"Keep kissing me like that," she whispered when he pulled back, "and I won't want to leave this room for many more years."

"That's kind of the point." His wink was playful but was underlined by nervousness. She patted his chest and then walked past him, slid open the door and went to the front where everyone was gathered.

"I want to say thank you for having my back," Selina said to the group assembled around her. Cal had brought Roman, Mina, Eric, Mack and Lucas, but Mack and Lucas were currently setting up closer to Caledonia so they had a command station ready when they arrived. It was less than fifteen minutes from their current location, but he felt like they'd fight for every mile. "Mina, do you have an update on the Randalls?"

"Yes." She shuffled some papers around and came up with one. "Randall Jr. is still in a coma. They can't pull the plug until a direct relative signs off on it."

"How convenient," Selina said, rolling her eyes.

"Exactly. I would guess that means Daddy Dearest has to sign the papers. Maybe from prison, or maybe he has to go there to do it. I wasn't able to find that information before we went dark."

"That may delay their arrival to Caledonia," Selina said, pacing in front of the small table.

"Or, he will leave his son in a coma and play the part for the cameras."

"While likely, that doesn't help us make a plan to take them down."

"But it does," Selina said, pacing the floor. "I tried to think of every way possible to sign that witness statement before Daddy Dearest has his hearing, but there's no way to do it without exposing me and the entire team. Instead, we'll just have to get him here and catch him in the act."

"You're thinking paperwork with his name on it, or...?" Mina asked, her head cocked in confusion.

"If it's there when the cops raid the house, then sure. In the meantime, our plan of action starts way before that."

"We're all in agreement that we keep the cops out of this," Cal said, his gaze darting to Efren, who nodded once.

Selina stopped pacing. "At least until I've gone in with the wire and gotten some confessions."

"Are you kidding me?" Efren exclaimed. "I didn't keep you alive for the last week to have you walk to your execution!"

"First of all, you didn't keep me alive," she said, stalking over to him. "We kept each other alive. That's what partners do. The other thing partners do is support each other. You're the one who told me to stop being afraid of being afraid and harness the woman who used to use fear as motivation. That's what I'm doing, so you can either respect that and participate in the planning of this mission, or you can disrespect it, stand here and keep your trap shut, but you can't have it both ways."

Mina was nearly biting her tongue off to keep from laughing by the time Selina stalked away from him, but he wasn't amused. What was she thinking? She was going to get herself killed, and none of their fancy guns or tactical skills could stop that from happening.

"She could shoot you on sight," Cal said, playing the devil's advocate. "Then we've got nothing to take them down with, their business stays open, and we all become Vaccaro's targets."

"You don't know my twin, Cal," Selina said, facing him. "She's dying to have it out with me. Ava wants to spew all her hatred for me before she kills me. She won't shoot me on sight. Will I get out of there alive? Depends on how good your snipers are." She glared at him, and he stepped back. Selina wanted him to take out her sister right in front of her?

"This time, I'll make sure she's dead, make no mistake." His words were firm, and even Cal lifted his brow. Efren didn't care what they thought about him and Selina at this point. Let their tongues wag; he had more important things to do, like protect Selina.

"What about Vaccaro?" Roman asked, putting his arm around Mina's waist. "It's bad enough that Secure One is on his radar. We don't want to be his targets."

Selina leaned against the table and crossed her ankles. Efren knew she wasn't nearly as relaxed as she looked, but she wanted the team to focus on what she was saying and not how she was feeling. He noticed she was always good at that, especially when an injury was in immediate need of care and the patient resisted. "Ava isn't the only target on the table. Anyone in the house is fair game as far as I'm concerned, including Vaccaro."

Cal's brows went up. "Now you're talking about a lot of death hanging over my head. I'm not sure I'm superbly comfortable with that."

"Let's be real here," Selina said, eyeing each one of them. "You've all been special ops at one point in your life. You all understand that sometimes we have to do bad things for the betterment of society. I can live with their deaths if the Snake stops hurting people for money. If it means the Snake stops destroying families and traumatizing children. If it means the Snake stops selling drugs that are killing people and making millions doing it. We are not above the law, but we do have a responsibility to the country, even if they walk around in their lives completely clueless about the things we're faced with in this job. That's how I want it. I've taken that burden on myself in the past and been okay with it because it meant good, honest, innocent people could continue to help others in the light, untouched by the darkness we see."

You could hear a pin drop in the small space when she finished speaking. Efren's chest had swelled the longer she spoke, and he stepped forward, finally joining the rest of the group. "She's right. It kills me to put her in danger, but she's right. Our entire mission at Secure One is to keep people safe. You've done that for a countless number of people already. We can do it again, safely, so we all go home at the end of the day. No one knows this man like Selina does, so I say we follow her lead." His gaze caught hers, and she smiled then mouthed "thank you." It was killing him inside to put her in danger, but he had told her to take her power back and let her fear motivate her. He couldn't turn around and tell her she was doing it wrong now. All he could do was make sure she was protected from harm, the one way he was best at.

Cal took a step forward. "Sierra is the mission commander. I expect you to have assignments ready when we get to Caledonia."

"Already done," she said, standing up and moving beside Efren. "Everyone has a specific role in making this a happy ending, but I've played to your strengths."

"Mina does not leave home base," Roman said without room for argument. "She's desk duty now for oh, at least the next six months." He put a protective hand on her belly and kissed her cheek.

Selina squealed and ran to hug her as everyone started talking at once. As Efren shook Roman's hand and hugged Mina, then pulled Selina into him, he was sure of one thing. He had found his home, and now it was time to protect it from evil.

Chapter Nineteen

The trip to Caledonia had been surprisingly uneventful, even if they had to hide in the back of a food truck headed for a Caledonia bar and restaurant. Selina would have ridden a horse if it meant they could end this decades-long feud between the Shannons and Vaccaro—at least the only Shannon who mattered. Ava may have sold her soul to the devil, but Selina would take a bullet before she did. Hopefully, the man sitting beside her would ensure that didn't happen.

Once there, they met up with Lucas and Mack, who had set them up in a small cabin just outside the Loraine property. They had set up a communications system to rival no other, only to learn they couldn't use it. Instead, they'd have to rely on flip phones to communicate. If one took too long to send a message... Selina hated to think about the consequences of that, so she shook it off. She had to keep her head in the game or she risked losing it to the Snake.

"I'm still not sure about the wire," Cal said as he leaned against a table in front of them. "You're the cop, so you know more than I do, but I didn't think you could submit a hidden wire as evidence."

"Depends on the state," Selina answered. "Minnesota allows it as long as one person in the conversation is aware of the wire." She pointed at herself. "In Illinois, laws are a bit tighter, but we aren't in Illinois. We're in Minnesota, and I'm technically still an officer of the law. That's why I'm wearing the wire and no one else."

"Run it down then," Cal said, motioning that she had the floor.

"The mission objective is to take Ava Shannon and Randall Sr. into custody after getting their confessions on tape to implicate them both in the counterfeiting operation."

"What about Vaccaro?" Roman asked from where he stood by Mina.

"Vaccaro doesn't come into play here," Selina said, facing him. "He won't return to Caledonia with the happily reunited couple."

"I'm aware, but the question was more geared at how do we stop him from coming after us?"

"We don't." Selina turned and leaned on the table to look them all in the eye. "Once we have Randall and Ava in custody, Vaccaro will cut all ties with them and anyone around them."

"I don't buy it." Roman shook his head with his lips in a thin line. "He's had thugs out searching for you for over a week now, and if this counterfeiting operation is as important as you say it is, he'll be looking for revenge that we shut it down."

Selina held her finger up as she stood. "We aren't shutting it down. We took two people into custody. We didn't burn down the house. He'll have that place cleaned out and the operation moved faster than we can book

Ava and Randall into jail. At that point, he slithers back to Chicago never to be seen again." She glanced at all of them one at a time and could see they didn't believe her. "You're going to have to take my word on this, team. I've known Medardo my entire life. I've seen how cold, calculating and evil he is. One day you're his favorite person in the world and the next you no longer exist to him. Are there thugs hunting me right now? Yes, but not at Vaccaro's direction. Ava is behind all of this. I'm surprised Vaccaro bought in, but then again, I'm not. Ava can be—" she motioned around in the air for a bit as she searched for the right word "—convincing? Relentless? If Ava Shannon wants something, she gets it. Right now, she wants me dead."

"Well, she's not going to get that," Efren growled from the corner.

Selina shook her head. "No, she's not, but we can let her think she is. Imagine her face when I waltz through the front door and into the study while they drink to Randall's release."

"She could have a gun," Lucas pointed out. "Then what?"

"Then I put my hands in the air and start talking. I know her. She will not shoot until she's had a chance to spew all her hatred at me. I'm the root cause for everything that's wrong with her life." She added an eye roll to assure them it was sarcasm. "Besides, if she gets trigger-happy, we'll have people in place who have a faster trigger finger than she does."

"That makes it complicated." Cal's grimace was felt by all of them, including Selina.

"That makes it attempted murder on her part and self-defense on mine. Case closed."

Eric looked up from his notebook. "What happens if you don't get anything incriminating on the wire?"

"We take them into custody anyway," Selina said with a shrug. "Then we call in the cops and let them tear the place apart to find the evidence they need to send them to prison."

"Where Vaccaro will get them out again?" Mina asked, a brow raised.

A sigh escaped Selina's lips. "Not likely. Again, Vaccaro has a line, and if we capture Ava and Randall, he will be done with them. They will pay for his crimes, which is always the way he likes it."

"Even if the cops come in and take the evidence before he gets there to get it?"

"I assure you, there will be no information in that house proving Vaccaro is involved in the scheme, just like last time. Randall went to prison, but Vaccaro was never even mentioned, even though we all knew he was behind it. The same thing will happen this time. The only way we could get Vaccaro for the counterfeiting is if Ava or Randall confirm it on tape. Even then, his lawyers will get him off."

"And if they both end up dead?" Lucas asked.

"Then we turn their cameras back on after I walk out the door and we walk away. Someone will find them and assume Vaccaro took care of his problem. Case closed."

"Except that the evilest one of the three is still walking around sucking air and ruining people's lives," Eric hissed. "I don't like that idea."

"You were a cop, Eric. You know that we can't get all

the bad guys. All we can do is our best and let the law take care of the rest."

"We aren't cops, though," Efren said. "If I think for one second that woman is going to get trigger-happy, she's going down. Messy or not, she's going down. I don't like any of this."

"Neither do I," Cal agreed. "Like it or not, we're between a rock and a hard place. We can't call the cops in since we have no proof of the operation being moved here. They can't get a warrant on 'we think this is what they're doing.'"

Selina shook her head. "There is no rock or hard place here, Cal. There is only one choice and we've made it. I will reprise my role of Eva Shannon long enough to take my twin and Randall down, and then Eva dies again."

"As long as Selina lives," Efren said between clenched teeth as all the heads around the table nodded.

She gave the final nod. "I apologize for putting you all in this position. If I could do it over, I would, but all we can do now is play the hand we were given."

"Don't apologize to us," Roman said with a shake of his head. "We've all done much worse things for the betterment of the world than what we're facing here tonight. My conscience is clear. It will be clearer if we can get Vaccaro, but two are better than none."

"With that decided, it's time for assignments." Cal pushed off the wall where he was standing and walked to the center. "You must memorize what Sierra tells you. I want no written evidence." Cal pointed at Selina's notebook. "Once the assignments are given, Mina will burn that."

"Ten-four," Selina said, spreading the notebook open on the table. "Let's walk through it."

As she handed out assignments and went over the plan of attack, Selina couldn't keep her gaze from drifting to the man who sat with his lips in a thin line and his arms crossed over his chest. He wasn't happy. Neither was she, but she understood one thing he didn't. If they ever wanted a chance to be together. To really have the chance to make a life together, then Ava had to die. Selina would squeeze the trigger without hesitation if she had to, and all she could do was pray he would do the same.

AVA SHANNON IS on the property.

Those words had sent a chill down Selina's spine when the scout team had reported in. They were surprised to find her look-alike sitting in the den sipping sangria when they did a sweep of the property. Like it or not, she had to act now, even if they all said it was too dangerous. If she could apprehend Ava, and then do a video testimony to send to the judge before the trial tomorrow, she could keep Randall in prison and send Ava there, too. Maybe she was being too idealistic, but she was using those ideals as her motivating factor. It was time to bring all of them some peace. If the only way to do that was to clash with her twin, then so be it.

Selina lifted her shirt, threaded the black leather belt through her pant loops, and buckled it in the front. There was a small recorder inside the buckle with an antenna running through the belt. It was voice activated, so it should easily pick up any conversation she had with her twin face-to-face. Since they wanted to avoid a digital signal, she couldn't wear a transmitter that would send a signal back and allow Mina to listen in. It would be all on her to get the audio they needed to put Ava behind bars with her husband. This was one time she was lucky that they had to go low-tech. The team didn't see the bigger picture, but she did, and the picture was ugly. It would be up to her to erase the past and start over.

Selina grabbed a secondary voice-activated recorder to ensure she got the recordings she needed. It was the length of a paperclip and slid into her pocket without leaving an outline on the material. She positioned her concealed holster at the back of her pants and tucked a small 9mm into it. She wasn't going in unprepared, and wasn't afraid to use the gun if push came to shove, and it just might. Her only goal was not to put that decision or action on any of her friends, especially Efren. "I killed for you" didn't feel like a winning basis for a healthy relationship.

Were they in a relationship, though? That was a question she couldn't answer without consulting Efren. She suspected any theoretical relationship they may have had would be destroyed when she left this cabin. It couldn't be helped. Selina was the only one who understood how volatile her twin was and how any plan wholly depended on Ava's choices, not theirs.

Knowing Ava was here meant the plan disappeared, and instinct kicked in. The Shannon twins were finally in the same place again, and in an hour, this would all be over. If they waited until after the trial and planned the mission down to the very last detail, it would be too late. Selina would text them she was going in right before she approached the front door. She felt bad that the team would have to scramble to get into place, but she'd tried to reason with them. Once again, they all disregarded her knowledge—despite the lack of their own—when it came to her family. She planned to buy them time by talking to Ava to get all the dirt she could on Vaccaro and Randall.

More than likely, Ava was at the house to destroy anything tying them to the counterfeiting operation. Once that was done, she would return to Chicago to join her husband before they disappeared for good. Selina couldn't risk it. Her past was her past, not the team's, and she would do whatever she had to do to protect them even if that meant dying. That was a real possibility, and even though Efren refused to address it, Selina was honest with herself at all times. These could be her last few minutes on this earth. She'd fight like hell to make sure that didn't happen, but if it did, she was taking Ava down with her.

The only thing she regretted was not kissing Efren before he left to scout out his sniper position, and not whispering three words in his ear after the kiss ended. She'd hold on to the emotions and those words, using it all as motivation to walk out of that house alive tonight. Efren may not want to hear it, but if she made it out, she'd tell him anyway. For the first time in her life, she'd be honest with a man about her feelings, even if he rejected her. And he might. She wouldn't blame him if he did, either. She was breaking his trust by going rogue, but what none of them understood was, she had no other choice. It was now or never if they wanted to apprehend Ava Shannon and put this to rest.

She slid her arms inside the sleeves of her Secure

One jacket and zipped it to cover the holster and the belt. After slipping past the closed bathroom door, where Mina was cleaning up, she slid out the door of the cabin silently. This would be the shortest and longest walk of her life, but one way or the other, the game would be over tonight.

Chapter Twenty

Efren swung through the cabin door and immediately switched out his all-terrain sole on his blade for his spiked sole. He'd found the perfect spot that would allow him to cover Selina when she was inside the house. He was more than surprised when he looked through his scope, and Selina's face stared back at him. He had to remind himself that the woman inside that house was nothing like her sister. Selina had a soul and she wasn't afraid to do the right thing, even when the right thing was the hardest thing to do.

Temptation had called to him when he had Ava Shannon dead to rights under his rifle scope. He could have ended the whole thing right then and there, and the desire to squeeze that trigger and make it look like an assassination so they could all go home was almost overwhelming. Instead, he did the right thing and took his finger off the trigger. The satisfaction he'd get in taking out Ava Shannon would be short-lived when he screwed up the rest of the mission by not hearing what she had to say.

"Selina?" he called, walking to the back of the cabin where several beds sat in a row. This was obviously someone's hunting cabin, as it was well cared for but utilitarian.

There was a figure on one of the beds, but it wasn't Selina. "Mina? Are you okay?"

"Hey, yeah," she said, sitting up and rubbing her eyes. "I was just catching some sleep. I was sick earlier, and the long hours are taking a toll on me. We couldn't have picked a worse time to get pregnant."

Efren chuckled as he leaned against the door. "I didn't know you guys were trying."

"We weren't," she said, sliding her leg into her prosthesis. "It was, what do you say, a happy surprise? Heavy on the surprise in the beginning. Our work doesn't lend itself to having a family, so I'm glad Cal is starting the new cybersecurity division *and* hired Sadie. She's going to be a godsend in more ways than one."

Efren held his hand out to help her up. "It's a great idea, honestly. We have more requests for cybersecurity than we do physical security now. Cal is lucky to have you at the helm. You're the reason it will be a successful endeavor for Secure One."

Mina playfully leaned into him. "You are good for my ego, Efren Brenna. As soon as this mission is over, I'll start looking for others to join the team. We'll have to recruit, and how we live at Secure One will be a tough sell, but if I can build a solid core team, we can always expand if needed."

"You mean like satellite offices?"

"More like the way Elliot works security around the upper portion of Minnesota. We'd have people who live off Secure One property who can go into businesses and fix systems that have been hacked, then build new security in. Remote, but still doing Secure One business."

"So needed, too," Efren said as they walked back into the main room. "Do you want me to flip through my Rolodex to see if anyone is looking for a change?"

"Yes, thank you! You have connections everywhere, so I know Cal would appreciate it as much as I do."

"No problem, I'll do it as soon as we get back to base." He paused and glanced around the empty room. "I thought Selina was staying with you and out of sight."

"I did, too. After I horked my guts out for fifteen minutes, I passed out on the bed. I thought she was out here."

Efren got a bad feeling in the pit of his stomach. "Did anyone report back what we found at the house when we did our recon?"

"You mean about Ava Shannon being on the property? Yeah, Cal, Mack and Roman checked in to let us know. They wanted us to arm ourselves but stay in the cabin. Selina argued with them for a while before they left again."

"What did they argue about?" A bad feeling filled the pit of his gut to overflowing.

"Honestly, I was sick, but I think it had something to do with them not listening to her?"

Efren cursed and ran for the back where they'd set up a makeshift equipment area. It didn't take but a second for him to see that her jacket and boots were missing. He jogged back to the front of the cabin. "What kind of wire is Selina wearing into the house?"

"We decided on the belt recorder. It's voice activated, so she doesn't have to worry about it not coming on when she needs it to." Mina pointed at the table but then cocked her head. "The belt is gone."

Efren cursed again. "She's going in alone tonight."

"You're jumping to conclusions, Efren," Mina said. "She's probably just out getting some air and you missed her on the way in."

"She's out getting air after Cal told you to stay hidden? No, she's going to have it out with her sister before we have anything in place to protect her—"

He was interrupted by a sharp report that had him jumping in front of Mina. When he realized it was too far away, he grabbed his jacket and ran for the door. "Text Cal! Tell him Selina's inside that house."

Efren pumped his legs as fast and as hard as he could as he ran to where his rifle was hidden. That shot could mean it was too late, but he had to try. He wanted to plow through the house's front door, grab Selina and then shake her silly for going off alone, but he couldn't risk it. For all he knew, Selina was the one to do the shooting, so it was better to get in place and assess the situation than go off half-cocked, the same way she had.

He scrambled up the ladder against the small shed, then army-crawled toward where he'd left his gun. The entire time he prayed to anyone listening that when he looked through that scope, the twin he loved was still standing. He'd planned to tell her how he felt before the mission, but now he was glad he hadn't. This little stunt was proof that trust was easily broken and that losing someone you love can happen in the blink of an eye. He couldn't, wouldn't, get involved with someone he couldn't trust, and Selina had proved that here tonight. She was the mission manager. If she'd wanted to change the plan, she could have easily called everyone in and prepped them for the change, but she hadn't done that. Instead, she decided she would handle this herself, without so much as the courtesy of a heads-up, and that told him all he needed to know about Selina Colvert.

SELINA SLIPPED THE phone in her pocket after texting the team. Get in position. I'm going in. Six words that would shape her future from here on out. She'd either walk out alive or be rolled out dead, but either way, this nightmare would be over for the rest of the team.

After a deep breath in and out, she walked to the front door, assured by the team that there were no cameras they could see on the house's perimeter. She found that odd at first until she remembered they had to fit into small-town Caledonia, and you don't do that by making your house a fortress. Selina had no doubt there were cameras somewhere, so rather than ring the doorbell, she tried the knob, not surprised when the door swung open. Her twin was expecting her. Good. That meant she wanted to talk. If she knew Selina was here and wanted her dead, she would have done that already. No, Ava wanted to have a chat with her, so she'd welcome her to her home.

Selina strolled through the house leisurely, giving the team time to get in place after getting her text. Before long, she found her twin, a replica of herself, sitting on the couch in a small den.

"Well, well, if it isn't big sister," Ava said without standing. "So glad you could stop in. I'm sure you've been dying to know how I'm still breathing. Considering, you know, you shot me."

"You don't give me enough credit, Ava," Selina said, inching her way into the room, but standing to the side of the window, just in case Efren needed a clear shot. "It's not hard to put your return from the dead squarely on Uncle Medardo's shoulders."

Ava smiled, and it chilled Selina to the bone. They may share the same features, but Ava's twisted into evilness with every expression. "Good old Uncle Medardo. We aren't blood related, but he's been better family than my own. He's taken care of me and made sure I had a roof over my head all these years. That's more than I can say for you."

"Considering I thought you were dead, I'm unsure what you expected me to do."

"Funny how that turned out. I thought you were dead, too. For over seven years, I lived in bliss, knowing I had not only done the heavy lifting to get rid of our father, but you had fallen to your untimely death just days after mine. Maybe I should say timely, at least as far as I was concerned."

"You killed our father?"

"Of course. He had to go. Uncle Medardo was too loyal to him. Daddy needed to be out of the picture so I could take his place. Funny how that works. He sold me for the price of a debt, but in the end, he was the one who paid."

"The debt he incurred trying to make you happy!" Selina exclaimed, anger filling her as she listened to her deranged twin. "You're the problem, Ava."

"No, you're the problem, Eva. You keep turning up like a bad penny, which has to end. That's why about a year ago, I happened to be in Seattle on business for

Uncle Medardo. Did you know your old friend Kai Tanner lives there now? Well, not in Seattle, some little town
around there, but he wasn't hard to find."

"You saw Kai?" Selina asked with her hands in fists
at her side. She wanted to pull her sidearm and end this
right now, but shooting an unarmed woman was murder.

"Such a lovesick fool," Eva said, brushing at her skirt.
"He sure had a lot to say when he thought I was you,
though. A chance meeting, a couple of spiked drinks and
a roll in the hay gave me all the information I needed to
know that my intuition was right. Your fall off the cliff
was nothing more than a swan dive."

"Did Randall Jr. know you were alive?" Selina asked,
forcing her mind away from Kai and concentrating on
asking the right questions to get the answers they needed
to put her away.

"Of course he did. Howie and I were running the
operation here at the Caledonia house while he kept his
father's other businesses going."

Selina finally understood why Randall had shot her
in the tunnel. He knew his stepmother was still alive, so
when he came face-to-face with someone who looked
like her, but was working with the law, he knew it had
to be her.

"How did you manage to keep the counterfeiting operation going when Randall was in prison? He was the
brains behind the operation."

"Wrong," Ava said haughtily. "My husband is nothing more than a puppet who makes Medardo look good.
Medardo wanted to get rid of Randall before he even
made it to trial, but I talked him out of it. I showed him
the operation here and that I was the mastermind behind

its success, not Randall. Keeping Randall in jail took the pressure off me and let me continue with the business here, while keeping him somewhere safe for use at a later date, if need be."

"And suddenly, because I'm alive, now is the time to use him?" Selina knew she was getting it all on tape, and wanted to keep her talking for as long as she could before she had to face down the inevitable gun her twin had somewhere in this room.

"More like a lucky coincidence. You see, the business here has run its course, and Medardo has a different assignment for us."

Selina smiled with satisfaction. If they'd followed the original plan and waited until after Randall was released from prison, they would have missed their opportunity to take them down.

"That's why you sent all the goons after me?" Selina asked, refusing to splint her side despite the pain. There wasn't a chance in hell she would give Ava the satisfaction of knowing she'd hurt her. "So I didn't screw up your new assignment?"

"I sent the goons after you based on nothing more than revenge," Ava spat, standing to get in Selina's face. She dug her finger into her chest. "You tried to put me in the grave, so tit for a tat, big sister." Ava's eyes were wild as she shook with vengeance. "You always thought you were so important, so righteous. The truth is, you're just like me, but you hide behind a badge to make your revenge heroic."

"I didn't realize you were so close to Uncle Medardo," Selina said, the words sticking in her throat. "What's it like letting that snake make love to you at night? The idea makes me sick," she hissed, the sound loud in the room.

Ava hauled off and slapped Selina across the face, but Selina didn't flinch. "Don't you talk about him that way! He loves me!"

The report of gunfire was so close to Selina's left ear that it sent her spiraling backward for several steps. She righted herself and dialed in on the scene in front of her. Ava was on the ground, blood bubbling out of her mouth as Vaccaro stood over her with a gun.

"You talk too much." That same voice from childhood drove a shiver down her spine. It had been so many years since she'd had the displeasure to be in his company that seeing him again was doing weird things to her equilibrium. "For the record, I never loved you, but you sure were easy to manipulate with those three little words, you poor misguided woman. Your daddy issues were your downfall, but I happily manipulated them to my advantage. Did you hear the news? Randall Jr. didn't make it out of the coma. He passed just an hour ago. So sad." He shook his head as though he had a heart. "I suppose the news will come out in the morning that his father died by suicide in prison when he learned the news. What a sad, sad family you all were."

Medardo swung the gun in Selina's direction. "Speaking of sad families, how lucky am I to get a twofer? In my opinion, it's more than time to make sure no more Shannons walk this earth. All the bickering in this family is exhausting—first, your father, then your sister. You were refreshing, Eva. You never kowtowed to your father, and you always did your own thing. I could respect you as an adversary, but my respect has limits.

This whole mess has to go away." He motioned around the room with his gun while Selina slid her gaze to her twin. Blood pooled around her on the couch where she'd fallen. Blood no longer bubbled from her mouth, and her eyes were fixed on the ceiling in the stare of death. There was no doubt that this time, Ava Shannon was dead.

"Eva Shannon is already dead," she said, and Medardo snapped the gun and his attention back to her. "As far as I'm concerned, we can come to an agreement."

"An agreement?" The question was filled with curiosity, so Selina shrugged as though none of it really mattered to her.

"We both walk away from here tonight and forget the other exists. I have a new life now that I'd like to continue to live, so I'm happy to strike a deal with the devil in order to do that."

Medardo laughed the laugh she remembered from their Sunday dinners when she was a child. "You always could make me laugh, little girl. Unfortunately, I won't be able to forget you exist. You're far too noble to pretend that I don't exist, either. No, the only way to make sure my interests are served is to dispatch the Shannon twins and be on my way. Especially since this place is about to go up in flames. It's a shame there's no fire hydrant way out here. When the house becomes an inferno, they'll have no choice but to let it burn itself out."

Medardo smiled the smile that reminded her of the snake he was. His gun lowered to her center mass, and she had to make a split decision. Try to run or go for her gun. Before she could do either, Medardo jerked backward with a shriek.

They both looked down at his arm to see half of it had

been blown off, and the gun was nowhere to be found. Medardo grabbed his elbow as he fell to the couch next to her sister, blood pouring from the destroyed tissue.

"You shot me," he said, shock setting in. "I can't believe you shot me."

"I didn't shoot you," Selina said, a smile tugging her lips up. "You see, I have friends who don't take kindly to bullies who threaten other people. They shot you. I'm surprised it took them as long as it did, to be honest."

Selina pulled her gun from the holster and glanced around the room. "An inferno, you say?" She sniffed the air, and the scent of accelerant reached her nostrils. It was hard to distinguish it over the coppery smell of her sister's blood, but it was there, and she had to get out sooner rather than later. He probably had the system on a timer to ignite on his way out the door. "You know, they say in life, you get back what you put in." Selina aimed at his kneecap and pulled the trigger. Medardo yowled in pain, unsure what to grab with his only free hand.

"That was for stealing my innocence," Selina said, backing toward the door. She couldn't risk being in the house when it went up. She didn't want any of her team seeing the flames and running in to save her.

"You can't leave me here!" he screamed. "My bodyguards are just outside the door."

"Are they, though?" Selina asked with a smile. "I suspect they're taking a nap just like all the other guys you sent out to find me. When they wake up and discover the house on fire, do you think they'll come running to save you? I'm going to guess no. I can't think of a better place for you to die, Uncle Medardo," she said with enough venom to poison the man in front of her. "You see, I right injustices regardless of the consequences, and that is something I will continue to do while you rot in hell right next to my sister."

Selina smiled, turned and gingerly walked to the front door. One spark and this place was going up. She didn't want to be in it when it did. With a final smile, she tucked her gun in her holster, pulled the door open and slammed it behind her. She'd seen the spark, and as she ran for the woods, she heard the telltale whoosh of the accelerant igniting. It was then that she knew it was over.

Chapter Twenty-One

The team was back at Secure One and gathered in the conference room. Last night had been a blur, and Efren hadn't had a second to breathe since they'd pulled in, all in separate vehicles. They didn't have time to talk, much less argue, about anything that had happened if they wanted to be out of the area before the fire engines arrived. They'd emptied the cabin and been on the road in under fifteen minutes, which was when they passed the fire engines heading to the inferno on the outskirts of Caledonia. All of them had watched that house go up and knew there would be nothing to save by the time they got there. Not the house and not the people inside it.

"Well, that was not our finest hour," Cal said to open the meeting. All heads turned to Selina, who sat at the end of the table in silence.

"I accept full responsibility for that." She stood and pulled off her belt and tossed a small device on the table.

"What's that?" Cal asked, pulling it toward him.

"Proof, should we ever need it."

"Unless his bodyguards wake up and decide to tell the police all about their involvement with a Mafia kingpin, I doubt that will be necessary, but I'll log it in."

"No, you're going to listen to it. Now." She pointed at the computer Mina had in front of her, and Mina hooked up the small device and did some fiddling. When she was done, she glanced at Cal, who nodded. Mina clicked the mouse and the room filled with Ava's voice. They listened in silence to the information unfolding.

Efren couldn't help but notice the expressions on their faces as they took in and processed the information. He also noticed how Selina subconsciously grimaced when the first shot rang out and then how she flinched when Medardo howled. Efren had hit his target dead-on. He could have killed the man, but that wasn't his goal. He wanted to get rid of the weapon and give Selina the upper hand to get out of the situation herself. In the end, it hadn't mattered, since Vaccaro was now dust.

When the recording ended, Cal glanced up at Selina. "What were you thinking?"

Efren noticed Selina's jaw tic once, and she blinked several times before she spoke. "We're supposed to be a team, but not one of you listened to me. You heard her," she said, pointing at the computer. "She was leaving Caledonia and never coming back. Had we waited until after the hearing, they would have disappeared. As soon as you said she was in the house, I knew. She was waiting for me. That entire game, her showing up at the hospital and pushing us farther and farther south, was on purpose. She wanted me to die tonight, and her ego was too big to consider it would be her who died."

"You both could have died!" Cal exclaimed. "I can't even wrap my mind around what happened. Not only did you break rank and go rogue, but you put yourself and this entire business at risk! If anyone figures out that we were there tonight, I'm done. Do you understand me? This business is over. We have protocols and plans for a reason!"

"You're right," she said, standing and walking to the front of the room. "This is my fault, and I take responsibility for it. If I wasn't willing to, I wouldn't have done it. You will have no legal trouble from what happened tonight. There is nothing left, and if they figure out Medardo died in that fire, you won't see the FBI crying about it. As you heard, Randall and Randall are no more, so this case is closed." She lifted her lanyard from her neck and set it on the table in front of Cal. "I hereby resign my position as chief medical officer at Secure One. I committed too many inexcusable offenses tonight to be trusted as an operative again. I will clean out the lab of my personal belongings and head out in the morning. Thank you for everything. I mean that," she whispered as she wrapped her arms around the man in front of her.

Cal hugged her awkwardly, his gaze holding Efren's in a look of terror and desperation. Efren wondered if he wore the same look. Was he angry at Selina for what she had done? Yes. Did she put them in a tough position? Yes. Did he want her to leave Secure One? His head said yes, she was a liability they couldn't keep around, but his heart said he'd follow her wherever she went and that was his internal battle now.

Selina ended the hug and turned to the team. The tears on her face had clearly surprised everyone as they glanced at one another around the table. "I owe all of you my life, and that is something I can never repay. The only thing I can do is say thank you for everything and for understanding that all of this—" she motioned at the devices on the table as she wiped a tear away "—started long before I ever had a say in how any of it would end. For the record, it ended the best possible way, and that's because all of you took it on your shoulders to do the right thing by doing the wrong thing. I'll never again lose sleep knowing that Vaccaro is still hurting people and I could do nothing to stop it. We stopped it. We did the wrong thing for the right reasons. That's enough for me."

"That's enough for me, too," Lucas said, standing and saluting.

"It's enough for me, too," Roman said, following Lucas.

"It's enough for me, too," Eric and Mack said, standing and saluting.

"I won't lose any sleep tonight," Mina said, standing and giving Selina a smile.

Efren stood slowly, pushing the chair back with his knee and meeting Selina's gaze right before he walked out of the room.

SELINA BLEW OUT a breath as the man she'd fallen in love with walked out on her. She expected him to be upset, but she also expected him to act like an adult. She was right about only one, apparently.

"Give him time," Cal said, resting his hand on her shoulder. "He's stared fear in the face a lot over the last week, and came to the realization too many times that he might lose you. Quite a few of us in this room have gone through it. Right?" She glanced up to nodding heads. "Give him some time, and he'll come around. Now, about your job."

"I'll head to the med bay and clean out my things." Her heart was heavy now that she was faced with the realization that this team would no longer be her team. "If you don't mind, I'll need to take care of my wounds, too." She lifted her shirt to show him her abdomen, but it was Mina who gasped.

"How are you even upright?" she asked, coming around the table to look at her ribs. "You need a hospital."

"Nothing's broken." Selina lowered her shirt. "I'll tape up my ribs and fix my incision before I head out."

"You're not going anywhere." Cal handed her the Secure One badge back. "You may have pulled rank tonight, but in hindsight, you did what had to be done. We, as a team, failed to listen to you about a lot of things when it came to Vaccaro, and that's on us, not you. When the going got tough, you walked in and took care of business. Do I like having an operative on the team who does her own thing, whether it's right or wrong? No. We will have to talk about that, but I do like having an operative on my team who is quick on their feet, competent and perceptive. You're all of those things, which is what made you a good cop back in the day. I think it's time we move you onto the team as the valuable op that you are, as I know you've been unhappy in your position for some time now."

"You want me to stay?" She lowered herself to the table in surprise. "As an operative?"

"Yes, but we can talk about it later when we're all rested. Promise me you won't go anywhere until we've talked, and you've talked to Efren. He deserves that much if nothing else."

He deserved so much more, but suddenly, Selina wasn't so sure she was the woman to give it to him anymore. She understood how he felt, and couldn't pretend that she didn't. She'd betrayed him by going after her twin by herself. It was a chance she had to take for the betterment of the entire world, but whether he believed that or not was up to him.

Cal dismissed everyone with instructions to get some sleep and meet up in the morning for a debriefing once the news reports about the Caledonia house, and the two Randalls, started to generate.

"Mina, could I ask a favor?" Selina asked before the woman could walk out of the room. She didn't know how to ask her this question without looking like she didn't care about the man who didn't think she'd done the right thing.

Mina smiled and pulled a piece of paper from her pocket. She handed it to Selina without a word and disappeared with a wink.

Selina looked down at the paper and all it said was, *Kai Tanner, Cliff, Washington. 425-555-4577.*

BEFORE SHE LOST her nerve, she knocked on Efren's door and waited. Selina had followed Cal's advice and given him an hour before she followed him, but she wondered if even that was enough. What happened in the next ten minutes would direct Selina's life going forward. If she and Efren couldn't come to an understanding, she would leave Secure One, despite Cal insisting otherwise. While she had screwed up the mission, she had also done the right thing, and that was something none of them could argue with.

The door cracked open, and Efren looked out. "Not into talking tonight, Selina."

She stuck her hand in the door before he could close it. "How about listening, then?"

Selina heard his heavy sigh, but he opened the door the rest of the way and let her into the room. "I'm sorry." Those were the first words out of her mouth, and he lowered his brow.

"Are you, though? It doesn't seem like you were too sorry when you were defending your actions in the conference room."

"I'm sorry for breaking the planned mission," she clarified. "And I'm sorry you were put in the position to shoot Medardo. I'm not sorry that they're dead."

Efren tipped his head to the side in agreement. "I don't have a problem that they're dead either. I took out his hand to give you a chance to do the rest. I do have a problem with my trust being broken."

"I know." She stared at her shoes for a moment before she glanced up into his deeply troubled eyes. "When I made the decision to do it, there was no question in my mind you'd feel betrayed. The problem was, no matter what angle I argued from, no one was listening to me."

"Including me," he admitted with a sigh.

"I spent a long time with the team after you left, helping them understand that what I did put my life in danger, but I did that so that they'd remain safe. If Ava had disappeared, I shudder to think how long it would have been before she turned up again, but I do know we'd all be looking over our shoulder. I want you to understand that is the reason I chose to betray your trust and risk my life. Better my life than any of yours, considering this was my fight. Did I play into Ava's game? Yes. I bit hook, line and sinker into it, but there was no other choice. I just hope you all see there was no other choice." Her voice was barely above a whisper by the time she finished her impassioned plea. Her hands fell to her sides, and she lowered her head. "You risked your life to keep me safe this last week, and for that, I'm eternally grateful, Efren. I'm sure when you got that text that I was going in, you felt as though it had all been for naught, but it wasn't, I promise. I will continue to do good things to help other people because that is who I am."

"Wait. Text? You sent a text?"

"Of course I did. I sent it right before I went in to tell you to get into position. How else would you know I was going in?"

Efren gripped her forearms gently and held her gaze. "I didn't get a text message. I was in the cabin with Mina and heard the first shot. I ran like a man possessed to where I'd left the rifle and looked through the scope to see Vaccaro holding the gun on you. You don't know how badly I wanted to end him."

"Why didn't you?"

"You needed to take your power back. You needed to be the one who made the decision you could live with. Doing anything else was being a hero you didn't need. That's why."

"I love you, Efren," Selina said the words in a rush of breath and tears. Her lips trembled as she tried to form words, but she hiccuped and had to start over. "You were the only thing on my mind the entire time I was in that house. How mad you were going to be at me and how I was going to lose you, but how I had to protect you. I had to protect you from those people so you could continue to help others. My decisions tonight meant I would lose you, but I couldn't leave Vaccaro on your doorstep for the rest of your life. That would have been wrong and the exact opposite of what it means to love someone."

Efren ran his hand through his hair as he stared at her. "You went into the house for me?" Her nod was shaky as she sucked up air, but she didn't speak, just lowered herself to the bed and tried not to sob.

He didn't say anything, just paced back and forth in front of her with his hands in his hair until finally, he joined her on the bed and tipped her chin toward him. "Do you know how I know that I love you?" Her eyes widened, but she didn't answer. "I let you see my leg. I made love to you without my prosthesis. I let you see me. The other night in the cabin was the first time I let anyone see me in twelve years. That's when I knew that I loved you."

"You love me, too?" Her voice was shaky, but she noted a little hope in the words.

"Probably since the first day you made a snide remark about my ability to guard someone. Do I love what you did tonight? No. Can I respect it for what it was? Yes. Do I ever want you to do something that stupid ever again? No. No. Never. Do you understand me?"

He had grasped her upper arms and held her so close she could feel his warm breath on her cheek. "Never again," she whispered.

"Did you really quit?" he asked, his gaze holding hers as their noses touched.

"I tried, but Cal wouldn't let me. He said we're going to talk about it tomorrow, but as long as I don't go rogue again, I earned my spot as an operative. I may take it, I may not. I'll talk to him first and then decide. That is, if you are willing to continue to work with me despite what happened between us."

"Despite what happened between us? Do you mean making love to you? Kissing you? Loving you?" She nodded against his forehead, and he smiled. "I'll only continue to work with you as long as we can still do those things, Selina. Do you think we can still have a relationship with all the baggage we carry?"

She gazed into his clear, open, accepting eyes. "I'll carry yours if you'll carry mine."

"That sounds like a mission we can work together on."

"Are you okay with knowing I can't have your child?"

"You're all I'll ever need in this life. Our lifestyle doesn't lend itself to little ones, and I'm okay with that if you are. I love you, Selina." He lowered his lips to hers.

"Not as much as I love you, Efren Brenna," she said against his lips right before he captured them for the first kiss of the rest of their lives.

Epilogue

Selina flipped through the news stories about the death of "known Mafia kingpin Medardo Vaccaro." It had taken authorities almost a week to identify the bodies in the house. The fact that it took so long told her that Vaccaro's bodyguards had indeed dipped rather than try to rescue their boss. Conspiracy theories were already rampant less then twelve hours since it was determined that the body found in the charred home in Caledonia was Vaccaro. The second body found next to him had been identified as Ava Shannon, a woman the world thought was already dead. While Selina's bullet eight years ago hadn't killed her twin, it had done enough damage to her heart that she required a pacemaker and defibrillator to keep ticking. Those devices were registered to the patient, and that was how they determined which Shannon twin had been found dead…again. As far as Selina was concerned, Eva Shannon was dead and she was happy to let it remain that way.

True to his word, Vaccaro had taken out both Randalls as well. To think Randall Sr. was so overcome with grief about his son that he hung himself with his bedsheets in his cell just hours from being released. The first thing Secure One had done was make sure that the only living Loraine son, Victor, was still alive and well in Bemidji, where he was recovering from being kidnapped by his brother just a few weeks ago while trying to save his fiancée. They were fine and rejoicing that Vaccaro, his father and his brother were dead. Now he could live an everyday life with Kadie and his son without leaving Bemidji. Since the Loraine home was now empty, they'd sell it and use the money to start their life together. Selina had never been happier to hear that something good would come from this debacle. Sadie, Kadie's sister and aunt to Houston, was even more thrilled. She worked at Secure One now as the chef, but if her sister and nephew remained in Bemidji, she could maintain her relationship with them easily, which was important to her.

There had been multiple times over the last week when she had to stop and ask herself if she had done the right thing. Each time, she got another sign that she had, so she decided to bury it in the box where she kept all the memories of her life as Eva Shannon. All but one part, that is. There was a thread dangling that would have to be tied up, but she had yet to find the courage to dial the number Mina had given her.

Cal had come to her a few days ago to talk about her job. He began by apologizing for treating her as an afterthought when the business took an unexpected turn. He admitted he should have asked her if she was comfortable caring for the women who had found their way to Secure One for safety, and not assumed she was a robot who could continue to care for them without help or someone to talk to about what she was going through as their caregiver. Selina had taken some of that respon-

sibility on her shoulders, as she could have spoken up
and told Cal of the toll it was taking.

In the end, he offered her a full-time operative position, which, after much thought, she'd turned down.
After the last case, she realized she was far more valuable to the team as a floater. She would remain the chief
medical officer at the compound, ensuring the men were
healthy and eating correctly by working with Sadie.
When they went on cases, she would also go, using the
mobile command as her home base where she would be
their medic or jump in as an operative if the occasion
called for it. She would also be the medical informant
for the new cybersecurity division. She'd help out when
something came up with a medical clinic or hospital that
the team needed help translating. It was a lot of hats to
wear, but that had been her life for as long as she could
remember, and she wouldn't want it any other way.

"Selina?" She turned and made eye contact with the
man who had been there to hold her up through each new
revelation over the last few days. Efren had spent some
time in the med bay with her. His limb had been damaged more than she was happy with, but he assured her
he had hurt it worse in the past. He came in for treatment
of the skin twice a day and was unfortunately using his
fancy wheelchair rather than his prosthesis at the advice
of his medical team. He took it unexpectedly well when
she told him he had to stay off it if he expected the damaged skin to heal, which told her that it was bothering
him far more than he was letting on.

"Hi," she said, walking to the door. She bent down
and kissed his lips in a work-appropriate buss. "Did you
need something? How's the limb?"

"My leg is fine, but Cal sent me down to get you. He needs you in the comms room. I'm here to give you a ride."

Her laughter filled the hallway after she locked the med bay door. "I can walk, but thanks."

Efren grabbed her hand and pulled her down onto his lap. "I know you can walk, but if you walk, I don't get the pleasure of having you on my lap." They wheeled down to the comms room where she kissed him and then hopped off his lap, walking into the room.

"Cal?" she asked, but the room was empty. She turned back to the hallway. "I thought Cal wanted me."

"He did, but he also wanted you to have some privacy, so he sent me to get you. Sit." He motioned at the chair in front of a bank of computer screens.

She took the chair and he rolled over, hitting a button and waiting until the screen illuminated. Selina's gasp was loud when the face staring back at her was the only happy part of her past.

"Kai!" she exclaimed, leaning in closer to the screen.

"Eva," the man said, his voice awed for a moment until he held up his hand. "Sorry, Selina. I'm just so stunned to see you again."

"Same," she said with a smile. "I never checked your blog, I'm ashamed to say. I was too afraid to want a life I couldn't have. I was afraid I'd do something not to the benefit of my health. Yesterday, I spent the day going through your posts from the first ones to the last. Thank you for being so good to Zeus."

"He was my buddy," Kai said with a smile. "From the day you handed him to me, he never left my side. It was like he knew I was his only connection to you and he was my final connection to you. Until the day he died he made me walk him with the leash you left him with that day."

Selina had her hand to her heart with a smile on her face and tears in her eyes. "I never doubted that you would care for him better than I could in my situation. You did such great things as a team. I'm so proud of your accomplishments. Look at you running your own team. I always knew you could and would do it one day. That's why I left. Had I stayed, I would have held you back and put you at risk."

"I can see that now," he agreed.

"Listen, about the elephant in the room," she said, glancing at Efren, who slipped his hand in hers.

"It wasn't you," he said before she could. "She approached me in a dark bar, and I'm embarrassed to say I fell for it in the beginning."

"Don't be embarrassed," she interrupted. "My twin was manipulative and calculating. You didn't stand a chance."

"Still, part of me knew. All of me knew when she barely touched my dog's head, much less loved him up the way you would have. By then it was too late. She'd drugged my last drink with ketamine."

"So she got her answers, but you don't remember a thing."

"Nothing other than bringing her home and then waking up naked and alone, with this feeling of being gutted all over again."

"Kai, I can't begin to tell you how sorry I am. When I left, I thought she was dead. I didn't know she was alive until a week ago."

"That much I figured. Part of me knew that you would have somehow let me know she was alive if you knew. It wouldn't be hard for her to find your old relationships and leverage them, especially since I took Zeus. I was more than a little surprised when someone named Cal reached out yesterday."

"I wasn't aware he had." Selina rubbed her hand on her leg nervously. "I was going to, I wanted to apologize for Ava. I just had to build up the courage I'd need to see you again."

"You always were my one who got away, but I hear you've found the one you're meant to be with."

"This is Efren Brenna. He's the only reason I'm sitting here talking to you. The last few weeks have been tumultuous."

"From what I heard, you did some search-and-rescue of your own kind. At least that's what I understood from reading between the lines. Let me offer my congratulations on that search. It was more than time. I'm proud of you for staying in the light and fighting the darkness with integrity."

"I don't know about all that, but I'm glad their reign has come to an end."

"He's right," Efren said, kissing the fingers of the hand he held. It felt to Selina a bit like a power play for Kai, but she'd allow it considering what they'd been through. "Your integrity in the face of bad odds is the reason the country is a much safer place."

Selina smiled at him for a moment before she focused on the screen again. "Gosh, it's just so good to see you. I want to hear about the Cliff Badgers and how you started the team!"

"Let's just say you weren't the only one looking for a fresh start. This was mine. I won't bore you with the details, but let me say this, friend. If you two are ever looking for a new line of work, you've always got a place on my team."

Selina lifted a brow at Efren, who lifted one right back.

* * * * *

Don't miss the continuation of
Katie Mettner's Secure One miniseries when
Holiday Under Wraps
goes on sale next month.

And be sure to look for the previous books
in the series, available now wherever
Harlequin Intrigue books are sold!

Going Rogue in Red Rye County
The Perfect Witness
The Red River Slayer
The Silent Setup

HARLEQUIN
Reader Service

Enjoyed your book?

Try the perfect subscription for Romance readers and get more great books like this delivered right to your door.

See why over 10+ million readers have tried Harlequin Reader Service.

Start with a Free Welcome Collection with free books and a gift—valued over $20.

Choose any series in print or ebook. See website for details and order today:

TryReaderService.com/subscriptions